Blackshirt V

CW00524316

Roderic Jeffries

First published in 2017 by Endeavour Press Ltd.

Table of Contents

Chapter One

If Richard Verrell had not been taken in by an old, old trick, he would not have seen Janet again. And if he had not seen Janet...

Verrell had finished his latest novel with the feeling of a job well done, also that since the weather in England was in its usual state of rain and wind he might allow himself a holiday abroad. He chose the south of France and four days after he had left the funereal shores of Dover, drove his car into the small town of St. Tropez. There the sun shone. The birds sang. And fires were unnecessary.

Two weeks passed and regretfully he thought about returning to England since he had promised to be best man at a wedding. For the last night he decided to visit the casino some fifty kilometres distant, and there to spend the evening enjoying a mild flutter at the roulette table. That night the stakes were small, with Greek syndicates and exiled kings elsewhere. While the atmosphere was thus less tense it suffered correspondingly and Verrell found that after an hour's play he had had sufficient. He had started with five thousand francs, suffered more losses than wins, and there remained but four one-hundred franc chips before him. What's the date today, he thought. Fourteenth. He placed the chips on that number, and rose from his chair, ready to leave.

The croupier called out. The last bet was hurriedly placed. The wheel spun, the ball thrown in counterwise, and all eyes watched the small band of whirling colour.

"Fourteen," called out the man.

A woman had already taken Verrell's seat, so, excusing himself, he reached over and collected his winnings. Fourteen thousand francs. Ten one-thousand franc chips, the rest in smaller denominations. Verrell grinned. Without hesitation he placed a thousand-franc chip on twenty-eight.

Three minutes later he was collecting thirty-five thousand francs. By some grape-vine the news of his second successive win had spread and a small crowd were eagerly watching. This time he put ten thousand, the limit, on thirty-six. As he did so somebody nudged him in the back. He half turned and a man apologized profusely, and elbowed himself even nearer the table.

"Thirty-five," the croupier called out.

Verrell scooped up what he had already won and turned to leave, content to rest on his laurels.

"Excuse me, *monsieur*, but aren't you going to collect your winnings?" It was the woman who had just taken his seat.

"Winnings?" he queried. "I placed the chips on thirty-six and — — "

"When you turned," she interrupted, "your coat-sleeve caught the pile and moved the chips until they half covered number thirty-five as well. At the time I thought that was what you intended."

"Are you certain?" he asked incredulously. As though in answer the croupier pushed over his winnings — one hundred and seventy thousand francs.

"Mademoiselle -?"

"Simone."

"Mademoiselle Simone, how can I thank you? But for you I should not have realized."

"Will you do me a favour?" She smiled.

"Of course."

"Put this thousand francs for me on any number you choose."

"Certainly — if you'll allow *me* to put the money on."

There was a slight argument, which Verrell won. He staked another ten thousand francs, one thousand of which was on behalf of Simone.

He chose number four... it won. The excitement was intense as another pile of chips was pushed across to the Englishman. He counted out thirty-five thousand and passed them to his partner, together with the stake.

"You seem to have the touch of Midas tonight. Often I have watched, yet never before seen anyone win more than twice running.' Her voice was as attractive as her person — yet he felt certain that she knew the hard ways of life.

"Are you carrying on?" she asked.

"No. Leave it at that. I guess that's about as far as I dare push things. Since you have brought me luck, will you have a glass of champagne with me?" Verrell would have welcomed her refusal. If he were to start early the next morning he needed a full night's sleep, and there was still three-quarters of an hour's drive before him.

"Thank you," she replied, giving him a hard, long look.

"I can assure you the champagne is not a hopeful gesture." He grinned.

She smiled in return, and as they moved towards the bar laid her hand gently on his arm. "It is not often that an unescorted woman receives an entirely disinterested offer. Now tell me where you are staying and how you enjoy this part of our country."

It appeared that Mademoiselle Simone lived in a small hotel on the outskirts of the town. Verrell offered to drive her home, but at her suggestion he agreed to walk back with her, since she insisted that it was such a small distance it would be silly to take the car — especially as the roads were very poor.

"If you don't mind, before we go I must phone a friend. I promised to ring earlier, but in the excitement of winning I forgot. I won't be long."

In less than two minutes she was back, and together they started walking towards the back of the town. The air was crisp, the sky clear and Verrell could feel his blood tingling with well-being as he strode along beside Simone. An amusing companion. Over the champagne she had told him several stories of the district that had made him roar with laughter — apparently the peasants were direct in their thoughts and speech. He was wondering how soon he might be back at his hotel when his thoughts were interrupted by a hoarse voice.

"Have you a match, *monsieur*?" A man shuffled up to them. A beret pulled down well over one eye, a chin darkened by two days' growth, and a greasy scarf round his throat merged into an equally greasy and grimy suit; his breath made Verrell wince.

"Yes." He flicked his lighter open.

At that second he realized he had walked into a trap. Behind him, he heard a slight crunch as someone came forward to tackle him from the rear. The woman was moving to one side. The man in front was breathing heavily, his body hunched, waiting for his quarry to be temporarily blinded by the light of the wick.

Verrell spun the wheel, but as the spark ignited the petrol he thrust the lighter in the man's face, at the same time leaping sideways. With a wicked hiss a shot-loaded bag cleaved the air where his head had been a second before. There was a grunt of surprise from the man behind. The garlic-eater had smashed the lighter into the gutter, cursing as his face was singed by the flame. With an oath he flung himself forward. Verrell brought his knee up sharply, felt it sink into the man's face with a sickening thud; then turned and caught the man behind with a right-handed punch that landed

7

squarely on the jaw. At that moment a hard weight caught him on the back of his head. He reeled; garlic-breath scrambled to his feet and caught Verrell a blow on the mouth; the woman again smacked down the butt of a small pistol.

"In his right-hand pocket, inside the coat, you fool."

"Shut up," snarled the man. He reached inside and ripped out the money Verrell had so lately won. As quickly as they had appeared the two men vanished, taking the woman with them.

*

"And how much did you lose, *monsieur*?" asked the inspector.

Verrell told him haltingly as he strove to keep the mist of pain from closing in.

"You can describe this woman?"

"About twenty-five; black hair worn fairly short; trim figure; pretty, but with a suggestion of worldliness, and rather —— " He groaned as the pain became more intense.

"I think, *monsieur*, it would be better to call a doctor, then tomorrow you may describe this woman more fully. For the immediate report I will merely say that you were going home with her." There was Gallic suggestion behind his words.

"I was not going home with her, I was escorting her to her hotel. I had every intention of coming away at once."

"You had?" murmured the inspector incredulously. He turned and regarded his subordinate. Then, "Pierre, call the doctor at once."

"Amazing!" muttered Pierre, before lifting the telephone receiver.

*

The doctor examined Verrell and allayed any fear of serious injury. However, the patient must remain under observation for several days, just in case. In the meantime he dressed the two wounds on the head, administered a mild sedative and prescribed immediate sleep.

The next morning Verrell awoke and, apart from a dull ache around the region of his neck, he felt sufficiently recovered to enjoy the humour of the situation. Blackshirt, the most notorious cracksman in England, had been duped, slugged and robbed as though he were a child of ten!

*

Two days later Verrell was up and about and arranging to return to his hotel at St. Tropez. He had wired his friend explaining the impossibility of turning up in time for the wedding, and, having thus squared his conscience, he decided to spend another week on the coast before returning. He was reading the morning paper when he heard his name called.

"Yes," he said.

"Monsieur Stephen Baker wishes to see you, sir."

"Stephen! Where is he?"

"At the desk, sir. Shall I ask him to come here, sir?"

"Certainly."

A man, of roughly the same age as Verrell, entered behind the boy and came rapidly forward.

"Richard, old horse! Read last night that you'd been assaulted and I don't know what! First I knew you were anywhere near this district. How are you? I must say you don't look as though you were about to peg out."

Stephen was an old friend of Verrell's, they had originally met at the club to which both belonged. He wrote poetry for pleasure, and painted scantily clad women in order to make a living.

"Thanks for coming along. It's all over bar the shouting, though I had a damned thick head for a day or two. What really worries me is that the first time I win anything worthwhile I have to lose the whole shoot."

"That'll teach you to keep to the straight and narrow in future. But what happened? Papers said you were escorting a young 'lady' to her house and— "

"Look here, Stephen, if you're thinking what I think you are, I'll punch your head in. I was merely taking her to her hotel. And the so-and-so's set about me." He described what had happened at greater length, and Stephen, taking a hint, forbore from humorous remarks on what seemed to be a touchy subject!

"You'll stay to lunch?"

"I'd like to, Richard, but I promised my sister to get back. The old cook's preparing something special. That reminds me, you've met Phillipa, my sister, haven't you?"

"Yes, last lady's dinner we had."

"Look. My sister's brought a girl friend down with her. The other day we got an invitation to a party which they want to go to. Absolute consternation as we were a man short, and then Phil suddenly read that you were handy. Wanted me to get hold of you and see if you'd care to make a fourth — as far as I can see they think your being bashed on the head is a direct intervention from providence — still you know what they're like."

"When is it?"

"The day after tomorrow, but before you say anything you'd better hear who's giving this do. I got invited because I know someone who knows somebody. But the hostess is the one and only Mrs. Varnes. I expect the name means something to you."

It did! For years now, Verrell had been making enough from his writing to live comfortably. But the restless urge for adventure, the thrill when danger threatened, the excitement of a battle of wits with the police, all resulted in his continuing to seek such excitement by being author by day — and cracksman by night. Blackshirt — a name the police dreaded. The name that meant yet another robbery without the suspicion of a clue. Blackshirt, who stole for the joy of stealing; whose code of behaviour had convinced the police that, at least, he was a sport. The man who would steal a sixpenny tiepin in preference to a valuable diamond, if the tiepin could offer the greater thrills. As Blackshirt, he kept track of those people who collected jewellery, or were known to have some particular piece, the exquisite workmanship of which made it a legitimate target for some future date. Mrs. Varnes was generally mentioned in the papers at least once a week. She was rich, immensely so. But where she had come from, or who she was before her marriage, nobody knew. Mr. Varnes was not such a mystery. As a Frenchman, he had amassed a large fortune during the occupation, which he had doubled soon afterwards when the allied powers were getting rid of surplus war equipment. He had been the subject of an inquiry as a collaborationist, but witnesses had either refused to speak or were missing. His name had been officially cleared; unofficially it remained what it had always been. Two years later he met with an unfortunate accident while driving a car. Again nothing was proved. He had married in 1946, and so his wife, after one year, found herself in possession of a large fortune, which enabled her to indulge in life with a capital L. She bought jewels with great rapidity and without taste, but included in her collection was a famous opal ring. And it was by this ring that Blackshirt knew Mrs. Varnes.

"Do you know her?" asked Stephen, as the other remained silent with a far-away look.

"I'm sorry. Of course I do, but for the moment the name had eluded me. She's the woman who gave that party some weeks ago which caused a rumpus with the local Communists."

"That's right. Well, she's invited us three and also a fourth if he would care to come along. Apparently it's to be a fairly big do, and a bit mixed, but people will get lost in the washing. Evening dress and all that, with breakfast in the morning, but, speaking personally, by the time three o'clock has come round I'm all for bed. Phil said she hoped you'd come along, and that if you will to have a meal at our place first."

"I'd like to very much, Stephen."

"Fine, that's all fixed. I'll give you the address, unless you'd like to be picked up?"

"That's O.K. thanks, I brought my car over."

"In that case, give me a bit of paper and I'll write it down. Come to us about seven, and afterwards Phil said that she would be only too glad to put you up for the night — or the morning."

"Many thanks, but I'll push on back to St. Tropey and collect the rest of my kit. Got to think of returning home to resume work."

"Work my foot!" said Stephen rudely. "Two hours a day, four days a week and then you make more than I ever have or ever will! "

A few moments later Stephen left. Verrell lit a cigarette. Had anyone been watching him closely they would have noticed his eyes light up with an expression of reckless excitement. Normally he would not have accepted the invitation. But it so happened that Mrs. Varnes was in possession of what was reputed to be the most perfect opal in the world!

11

Chapter Two

Phillipa's friend, Susan, proved to be a charming addition to the party, and the meal everything Stephen had promised so that the evening went with a zest from the word go. Stephen recounted some of the foibles of the advertising world, with particular reference to such portraits as displayed ladies' underwear. At that point his sister brought his conversation to an abrupt halt. After the meal they settled in the lounge, while the maid brought coffee, and the host poured out the liqueurs.

"Can't say who'll be there, tonight, Richard — last time we didn't know a soul, but then everyone else was in the same boat as far as I could see. Mrs. Varnes collects the most amazing set of people you could hope to meet in a day's march."

"Thank you," smiled Verrell.

Phillipa looked blank for a moment, and then chuckled. "For that much you're still included. There's something about you, Richard, I don't understand. You appear to be a very respectable man, the kind 'who make England' as people will have it. But I'm certain underneath you're not nearly so conventional as you'd have us believe. Every now and then your eyes have a wild and reckless look." She was only half joking.

"Ten to one he's wanted for bigamy by the police," suggested her brother.

"Don't be silly," interrupted Susan scornfully, "he's much too nice for that."

"Too sensible." Stephen handed Verrell a cognac. "Besides, you know the dire penalty for such a crime as laid down by one of Her Majesty's deceased judges?"

"No. But I suppose we've got to know."

"Two mothers-in-law."

In the ensuing laughter Verrell steered the conversation round to a description of the villa they were about to visit.

Having been unable to reconnoitre, he was anxious to gain as clear a picture of the lay-out of the house as possible. It would perhaps have shaken even Phillipa had she known that around his waist, in a belt next to his skin, was a collection of housebreaking instruments as perfect as man's ingenuity could devise. Made of hardened steel, there were few safes they could not open when handled by Blackshirt.

"How big is the house?" he asked.

Stephen answered. "It's big — and it's small."

"Very lucid!"

"Thank you. What I'm trying to say is that though the villa itself is bigger than most, the rooms are all so large that there can't be many of them. The ballroom takes up the whole of the south side, and off that you've got the dining room, nearly as large, and a sitting-room… that really is lovely."

"Gaudy, Steve, not lovely."

"My dear Susan, as I'm describing it, allow me to do so without interruption! The sitting-room is lovely. Then there's a study, but I've only seen that from the small room where we leave our coats. I haven't been upstairs, but Phil says the principal suite is really something."

"How many floors are there?"

"Three, so far as I know. The top one contains all the staff rooms. She keeps four or five maids, apart from the kitchen staff — must be nice to have that much money," he ended reflectively.

"I'd settle for her jewellery," said Susan. "Have you seen that rope of pearls she wears. Heaven alone knows what it's worth."

"Where on earth does she keep all those jewels? Darned dangerous to have so much wealth lying about."

"There's a safe in the library somewhere. She mentioned it last time we met. Said something about having it moved up to her bedroom where she could keep an eye on it. Absolutely gloated when she was telling us what she had. Indecent for any person to have that much! I wish someone would come along and pinch the lot — only I suppose it's all insured."

"Female love for you, Richard! If Phil had what the old woman has, there wouldn't be any of this talk about indecency." He glanced at his watch. "Come on, you people, time we were off. Invitation said ten and it's that already. Won't be there much before eleven by the time the girls are fit."

The two women left to get ready. Stephen went to a cupboard and brought out a box of cigars. Soon the air was fragrant with their smoke.

*

By twelve most of the guests had arrived; a dance band was playing the latest American and French hit tunes; while in the lounge champagne and a buffet meal were being served. Verrell had had several dances with his party, but after an hour or so had excused himself on the plea of a very slightly turned ankle. Since another man had joined the party, Verrell did not feel too many qualms at leaving.

Mrs. Varnes was in good form. There were one or two celebrities present but she was wearing at least three times as many jewels as they. Her little crowd of sycophants had assiduously paid court and told her how charming she looked. When she had been introduced to Verrell as 'the popular author' she had murmured 'of course' with such sincerity that it was obvious she did not recognize the name. Also that she was not interested. To Verrell she seemed overdressed and there was more than a hint that under her paint and powder there was a much older face, with lines other than those caused by old age — maybe, he thought, some of the things Stephen said about her were true after all!

From the lounge Verrell wandered into the buffet, where he secured a sandwich of *foie-gras* and a glass of champagne. From there he moved, apparently aimlessly, in the direction of the library. His hostess was wearing a mountain of jewellery, but not that opal ring!

The library was deserted. The overflow of coats and hats was neatly stacked on chairs, but the two maids who had been taking charge of them had disappeared. For a full five minutes Verrell walked round as though a casual sightseer, but during that time he had kept a careful watch on the two connecting doors. One led out to the passage along which was the ballroom, and during that time not one person had passed. The other door was shut and had remained so. The room was dimly lit, and when the time came he felt certain that if he extinguished the lights his act would go unnoticed. Carefully he memorized the position of the furniture.

The whereabouts of the safe was the next problem. Apparently it was an old one, and He had the impression that it would be fairly large. On that assumption, and since it was not in evidence, the safe must be concealed behind a fairly large covering. There was a group of paintings on the far side, none of which was large — they could be investigated later if it should be necessary. The most likely hiding-place was behind one of the two tapestries on opposite sides of the longer walls.

Leaning carelessly against the tapestry depicting a hunting scene, Blackshirt raised the glass of champagne with his right hand and gently sipped. Behind his back his left hand was tapping at the wall. The material was too thick to give positive results. In his lapel he had a pin and removing it he pushed it into the wall. It gave, slightly. Then, he held it up at eye level, as though he had just picked it up from off the floor. The point was not turned as it would have been if thrust against metal. Within five minutes he was convinced that the safe was not behind either of the tapestries. He examined the paintings, studying them from a distancc and close to, and every now and then carelessly nudged a frame. Again he had drawn a blank. Returning to the centre of the room he looked round.

The fourth wall, with the closed door in the centre, was lined with books. Books which looked as though they had not been moved from the day they had been carefully arranged on the shelves to justify the name 'library'. It was possible that part of the shelves was false. But as careful an inspection as Blackshirt dared give revealed no break in the woodwork, nor any fake books.

He shrugged his shoulders. Phillipa had said the safe was in that room. But it seemed more than possible that Mrs. Varnes, not for the first time, had been 'careful' with the truth. If the safe were not in this room then he must give up the idea of obtaining the ring. It would be impossible to search elsewhere as he had searched here. Besides if, for the sake of argument, the safe were in the main bedroom, he could offer no reasonable explanation for his presence there. He had turned to go, convinced that he might as well give up and enjoy the dance — as a dance! — when he paused. Something was worrying him. Some little fact, insignificant in itself, which had been appreciated by his sub-conscious mind and was now trying to express itself. Something to do with light. Then he had it. Whilst examining the wall at the far end containing the book-case he had passed the door in the middle without thought. But though it had a keyhole no light had shown through. Perfectly possible that this was due to a close-fitting key — or that the light was not on in the next room — but the house gave one the impression of having lights on everywhere.

There was no gleam either from beneath or above the door. It was locked. Five minutes later there was a 'click' as the lock opened. Blackshirt returned the skeleton key to the belt around his waist and then eased his numbed hands. He had been working with them behind his back, as he lounged against the door, and the strain had made the nerves in both wrists 'jumpy'. Behind the door lay a large and old-fashioned safe, of a type that should take him no more than five minutes to open. Smiling, his eyes lighting up with a reckless, daredevil expression, he returned to the dance floor. Later that night, or morning, when people were feeling tired, he would pay another visit to the library!

"What have you been doing?" asked Susan. "You look as though you'd met your best girl friend."

"You'd be surprised," he retorted.

"You're not kidding," she said, smiling.

*

It was four o'clock in the morning. Still too early for any of the revellers to leave. But late enough for most of those present to look tired. Stephen, aided by many glasses of champagne, had forgotten his earlier suggestion of leaving as soon as was decently possible, and was enjoying himself. Every now and then he upbraided Verrell for the small amount he drank.

"Come on, Richard, fill that glass up. You've been playing with it for over half an hour now. Forget what it costs in our beloved island and relax!"

"For goodness' sake don't encourage someone else to have too much."

"Who's had too much, Phil? Are you suggesting I?"

Verrell interrupted what had all the hall-marks of a family argument. "Is that C. H. James over there, by the door?"

"Who's he? Never heard of him."

"He's one of the members of the club. Writes for some magazine or other. Shan't be a moment, but I'm certain it was he. There's something I want to ask him." Verrell moved over to the door, while Stephen endeavoured to make out whom his guest was talking about.

Once outside Verrell moved quickly. The cloak-room was just before the short corridor leading to the library. When he arrived there had still been room to hang his coat there. From the pocket he removed his silk scarf. It was white outside, but when turned inside out became black; wrapped round his neck and tucked inside his jacket it hid his dress shirt and waistcoat. In his belt was a black mask. While he did not feel as safe in such clothes as in his famous black shirt he had deemed it safer to wear a normal dress shirt. He held the scarf loosely in his right hand. Making certain the rustle of a long dress passing the way he had lately come; then silence before the light was switched on again and three corridor was clear he moved out of the cloak-room in the direction of the library. With average luck in ten minutes the ring should be his.

At that moment a woman's scream echoed from the library. The light in the hall was switched off; there was a people, two of them guests and one the butler, came rushing forward.

Verrell's reactions had been instantaneous. He moved backwards and returned his scarf. Quickly lit a cigarette and then ran out of the cloakroom.

"Where was that noise from?" panted one of the guests.

"Somewhere over there." Verrell pointed vaguely in the direction of the library. They all rushed forward in a bunch.

In the centre of the room one of the maids was lying on the floor and at the sight of the others she screamed again. From behind more people pushed into the room.

"What's wrong? Snap out of it, girl, what's all the fuss about?" The butler shook her.

"The safe. Madame's jewels. Help, thieves."

They had been too intent on the girl to notice the rest of the room. But when they regarded the far end they saw that the bogus door was wide open, the safe likewise.

A small hurricane rushed past the group. It was Mrs. Varnes. With a cry she searched inside the safe, her face white with fear. She turned. "My ring, my opal ring, it's gone," she cried. Then sank to the floor in an excellent swoon.

*

Stephen always said that the party was an even greater success after that. But then he had secured a couple of bottles for his party, foreseeing events were likely to be protracted.

"My God! Richard, trust you to be in the thick of it. If anyone had to be near the scene of the crime, it had to be the one and only 'famous author, Verrell'. Now I suppose you'll write another of your mediocre stories with this as a background, and make a lot of money. Shouldn't be surprised if…" He stopped, realizing Verrell was not listening to a word, but instead was gazing fixedly at a guest some thirty feet away.

"Bit of a smasher! But I wish you'd listen to what I'm saying; been talking to you for five minutes now and you haven't paid the slightest attention."

Verrell turned. 'Tin sorry, what were you saying?" Stephen told him. But once again he did not take in the words. For the woman he had just seen was surely Janet… Janet Dove. Her hair was different. She had had it piled up at the back into a kind of bun. And, if his memory wasn't playing tricks, the colour had changed. But they were small differences — normal differences, he thought with a grin.

As if aware of his interest she turned, started, and for a moment glanced wildly about her. Then she regained her composure and with a last hard look turned her back on him.

It *was* Janet. And she had recognized him! The enchanting adventuress who had taken the Roselea rubies just twenty-four hours before Peebles and he had opened the empty safe. Who was bewitching woman one moment, and hard, unscrupulous crook the next. Yet in either role as charming a companion as one could wish to meet.

There had been a trace of fear in her eyes. Why? he asked himself. The answer was not far away... It had been a woman who passed him in the passage — rushed by from the direction of the library.

"Damned if I ever speak to you again, Richard."

"Do be quiet, Stephen," said Susan. "If he wants to think, why shouldn't he? No need to be so envious."

"I must apologize," said Verrell for the second time. "But I was thinking along the lines that you'd suggested. Wondering who has the missing jewellery. You know, it'll make quite a good plot."

"Why?" asked Phillipa. "You don't think any of the guests would do such a thing?"

"It was a woman who rushed past me in the corridor."

"So what? What about all the maids? You're a thoroughly vicious character, Richard; soon you'll be saying I did it!" Stephen was indignant.

"You don't wear skirts."

"Not that I haven't sometimes thought he'd look sweet in them," said Susan with a giggle.

Stephen's reply was cut short by the arrival of the police.

The guests were asked to remain in the ballroom. Two *gendarmes* stood by each door to make certain the request was observed. The servants were ushered into another room. The inspector remained in the library and called for Mrs. Varnes. She left the ballroom supported by a maid, and was gone a long time. The guests hung aimlessly round, some of the older ones unashamedly asleep.

A uniformed man entered the room after a hurried conversation with one of the *gendarmes*. "Attention, please, everybody." The slight hum of voices died down. Even Stephen replaced his glass on the table. The man repeated himself in broken English. "Will those gentlemen who first discovered the burglary kindly identify themselves."

Verrell stood up. Across the room two other men did likewise. The inspector consulted a notebook. "Thank you very much. Will you three please follow me." They did so. Behind them came one of the guards.

They were led into the library. The inspector had drawn a chair and table into the centre. A thin, sleepy man, evidently a clerk, was waiting to take down the evidence. Also at the table sat the maid who had discovered the crime.

The three were identified by the maid, though with evidence uncertain to a degree. Then by the butler. Verrell was asked to stay — his companions led out of the room.

After the preliminary questions had been answered, the inspector relaxed, smiled, and offered a cigarette.

"Monsieur Verrell, you say you were in the cloak-room when you heard the scream. Did you hear anyone pass outside the door after that moment, and before you moved into this room?"

Question after question for some five minutes — then he seemed to be satisfied. Verrell was asked to return to the ballroom.

Stephen asked several fatuous questions, but even he was becoming influenced by the atmosphere — one of annoyance that the evening had been cut short; and an earnest hope that soon everybody might be allowed to return home.

One hour passed and then the room came to life again as all the police officials entered. This time accompanied by two elderly women in overalls. The inspector spoke up.

"Ladies and gentlemen, I have been investigating the crime which has just taken place." He paused dramatically, then, "The criminal is still within the boundaries of this house. Therefore, with Madame Varne's permission and yours, I will conduct a search of those present. After which I hope it will be possible for all of you to go home. Now, if Madame will permit " He turned in the direction of the hostess.

"Hurry up and get on with this search. I won't rest until you find my ring. If necessary —"

"If the gentlemen will follow me," he took no notice of the interruption, "and the ladies follow my two assistants we will proceed as quickly as possible."

Later the report was complete failure. The opal ring had disappeared.

The hostess said good night to none. She retired to bed with a headache. The police departed leaving a couple of men with instructions to search the premises.

Verrell had been one of the first to leave. As quickly as he deemed prudent he gathered up his coat and hat, and, without a word to Stephen, entered his host's car and drove it round the drive until he had a full view of the porch. At almost the second he came to a halt, Janet walked out and straight across to a car parked opposite. She started the car, then, skilfully avoiding a bunch of people, drove away. Behind her, Verrell followed.

*

"Look here, old man, would you mind telling us just where and why you've been. Not, of course, that we mind! Oh no! We like to be kept waiting while our guest takes our car out for a jaunt to see the countryside by moonlight. If it weren't that Susan realized you also were missing I would have informed the police that my car had been stolen. You'd have looked damned funny if you'd ended up in gaol!" Stephen was annoyed.

*

Verrell drove up later that morning to the hotel to which he had trailed Janet earlier. He parked the car, entered, and walked up to the desk.

"I would like to see Miss Dove, please."

"What name, sir?"

"Miss Dove."

The clerk regarded a ledger. "I'm very sorry, sir, but we have no one of that name staying here."

"Maybe I have the name wrong. The person I want is staying here, I brought her back last night from a dance." He described Janet.

"I'm afraid we have no one like that here. You may see for yourself. We have no single English lady here at the moment, sir."

It was a check that he had half feared. Janet, realizing she was being followed, had driven her car into the car park of the hotel, entered and waited until he left, then returned to wherever she was staying. It was more than probable, then, that a night porter might be able to tell him in which direction she had gone.

"I would like to speak to the porter who was on duty earlier this morning."

"I'm sorry, sir, but I cannot get hold of him at the moment."

Verrell glanced sharply at the man behind the desk. He was playing dumb. He knew something but was not prepared to talk.

20

"How much did Miss Dove pay you to keep quiet?"

"I don't know what you're talking about. If you have nothing else to say, sir, I must ask you to leave as I am a busy man." But the man's eyes wavered at the word money.

Verrell said nothing. But he pulled out his wallet and withdrew a thousand-franc note. Twice more he did this. He laid the three notes on the counter.

The clerk licked his lips. His greedy eyes wandered from Verrell to the money. Suddenly he leant forward and lowered his voice, "*Mademoiselle* was generous. She gave me five thousand francs to divide between myself and Jacques, the porter, to keep quiet if someone like yourself should ask any questions."

"'And I am offering three thousand for yourself."

"Jacques would also need squaring."

Verrell smiled gently. "Perhaps I should see the manager and get the address of this porter. No doubt he would be interested when I tell him that his share of keeping quiet came to two and a half thousand." He had made a shot in the dark, but from the way the clerk winced and looked apprehensively around it seemed as if Jacques *would* be interested to hear what his full share was.

"Very well. Miss Dove left here over half an hour ago to catch the train for Paris." There was a note of triumph in his voice. He reached for the money. But Verrell was before him.

"Any forwarding address?"

"None. She said there would be no mail for her."

"What did she give you as her home address?"

"The Dorchester Hotel, London."

Verrell grinned wryly. He was willing to bet that in the circumstances that was the last place in London she intended to visit. She always had been a suspicious devil!

"When did her train leave?"

"Just five minutes ago, sir." It seemed to the clerk that the three thousand francs were fast disappearing. The thought stung him into some gratuitous information.

"It stops *en route* for twenty minutes, sir, to meet a connexion. If you hurried you might just be in time to make it.

Verrell thought quickly. There was something in what the man said. The distance was just under sixty kilometres. If he drove all out, and it was a good open road, he might just catch the train. Thanking the man curtly he left.

Verrell was a good driver, and his Healey sports model seldom dropped below eighty miles an hour as he raced for the station. As he approached the town he slackened speed, but on at least one occasion another driver hurled the epithet 'Sunday driver' after the fast retreating red car. At the station Verrell learned that he had three minutes in which to buy a ticket and board the train. He bought a first-class ticket, thinking that Janet, with her love of comfort, had probably done the same. His car remained in the station yard — where he hoped he would find it on his return. As he raced aboard the guard blew his whistle, and the train moved off.

At each compartment Verrell regarded the occupants. Towards the front he came to one with only two travellers. One was Janet. The other the detective who had investigated the case of his own robbery a few nights previously.

Chapter Three

Verrell paused before entering the compartment, his mind busy with a series of unanswerable questions. Why was the detective there? Was it a coincidence that he was in the same compartment as Janet? But that was stretching things too far. Did Janet know that the man was a detective? It seemed unlikely. He had not appeared at the villa the previous night, and was now in a nondescript suit. At the moment he appeared to be sleeping. In that case Janet was probably under suspicion. The police knew a woman had passed along the passage just after the safe had been found open. No one had said what evidence the maid had been able to give. But it might have been sufficient to enable them to get a lead. He was frankly grinning as he entered the compartment.

Janet turned from the window and smiled. He realized that she must have seen him board the train and was now trying to make the best of a bad job. The detective opened one eye. "Monsieur Verrell," he said in French — his English was non-existent. "How are you? Have you recovered from the blow you suffered? We tried to trace that woman and her friend, but... He threw his hands up.

Verrell was half watching Janet and he saw her start as she realized the import of the man's words. So she hadn't known that her companion was a detective!

"And are you returning to England?"

"Not yet. I had a telegram from a business friend asking me to meet him in Paris, and, since it is important, I've had to make this trip suddenly. Bit of a nuisance as I've had to leave my car at the station. I wonder if you know of a garage who could send a man along to collect it and keep it until I return?"

"Of course. You can send a wire at the next stop. Mention my name, they'll be especially attentive," he said complacently.

"Fancy meeting you here, Richard," said Janet ironically in English.

"How are you, Janet? I've often wondered how you were getting on. Did you have a nice holiday?"

"Excellent thanks, though of course the funds wouldn't last for ever."

Verrell whistled silently. If she had spent everything she had made from the sale of the rubies, then she must have lived for a short time the life of a South American meat exporter.

He offered his cigarette case. The inspector accepted. Janet refused. A moment later she left, saying that she wanted a cup of coffee.

"Monsieur Verrell, pardon me if I am personal, but do you know that lady?" The voice was sharp.

"Hardly go so far as to say I know her. I was at a dance last night, and my friends introduced me to her as a compatriot."

"Would that be the dance held by Mrs. Varnes?"

"Yes. Funny that I should be mixed up in another robbery, isn't it? Of course, you must have heard about it?"

"Yes. Can you tell me anything about this lady?"

"I'm afraid not. As I said, it was a case of an introduction and one dance. I was with a party, and after that I returned to them. The only other time I spoke with her was to say good night. You sound as though you were suspicious of her "

"Monsieur Verrell, I must reluctantly point out that I cannot discuss such matters. But you will understand that your answers to any questions I ask may be of the utmost assistance."

"Of course. I shall be only too glad to help."

"If I remember rightly, you were in the cloak-room... For a short while the inspector questioned Verrell, then lapsed into silence. He took out a battered pipe, filled up, and lit the tobacco. Then he spoke again.

"Just now I said I could not discuss the affair with you — but it becomes necessary that I should explain a little, for I should like your assistance. As you know, the maid was hysterical. Later she became rational. But all she could tell us was that the person she had surprised at the safe was a woman in a green evening gown. She did not see her face. Naturally we made a check on those wearing such colour dresses. There were three. This young lady was one of them — and, as you see for yourself, she returns to England very soon after the event. It may mean something, it may mean nothing. While Mademoiselle Dove has been here her baggage in the guard's van has been searched. I expect to hear the result soon. What I want to do now is to search her handbag, which I see she left behind, and that small case above. If you would be so good as to keep a look-out for her return from the direction of the refreshment car, I will do what is necessary."

Verrell's face clouded over. "I'm terribly sorry, but I don't think I could — "

"Monsieur Verrell. If the young lady is innocent, you will be helping to establish the fact — if she is guilty I am certain you would not wish to protect her!"

"Well, I — I suppose so." His face seemed worried. Inwardly he was laughing. Blackshirt being asked by the police to keep watch!

If the inspector should find the jewels then he, Blackshirt, would make certain the other did not keep the incriminating evidence; if they did not find it, then Janet must have the ring on her person... in which case...!

"If she should be guilty, mayn't she be hiding it now?"

"She is being watched by one of my men," he replied shortly. For the first time Verrell realized how thorough were the precautions.

"Now if you will please sit over there, with your back to the engine. From there you can see the length of the carriage. Tell me the instant she appears."

Verrell did as he had been requested. In the reflection of the glass he watched the other at work. First the small suitcase. Each article was emptied in strict order, then meticulously searched. When the bag was empty, the inspector tapped the lining all round. He grunted in annoyance, replaced the contents, and returned the case to the rack. Next the handbag. Here the contents were more varied, and in no order whatsoever. Powder compact, lipstick and a dozen oddments were carefully investigated, but the result was negative.

"Would you translate this letter for me, *monsieur*, it has no signature; unusual." He handed the paper over.

The note-paper was headed Locano Private Club, Wells Street, London, W.I.

I received your letter and can't promise anything until I see you. Maybe we can come to an arrangement. When you arrive ask for me, and one of the boys will show you up. But remember, no funny tricks this time.

"It is a circular letter advertising a night-club," said Verrell. The other was satisfied. He replaced the letter in the bag, the bag on the seat.

"If she has it, she is a clever one," murmured the inspector, almost to himself. He puffed hard at the pipe.

There was a knock at the door and a tall, thin man beckoned. The inspector grunted, went outside. A moment later he returned, his brow furrowed.

"Not in her trunks," suggested Verrell carelessly.

"No. If she has it, it leaves but one place. Her person. Before she boards the ship she will be searched. Then if no ring — we must cross her off." He was obviously worried. The two other green evening gowns present had been well-known local inhabitants, eminently respectable. If this lead should peter out, he could foresee many sleepless nights.

Verrell was also thinking quickly. Janet had the ring. Of that he was certain. It was not in her luggage. Then it was on her person. But where? And how was he to gain it? Failing everything else he would warn her, so that she could dispose of the evidence. But his immediate aim was to secure the ring for himself. Of course, he could always tell Janet that he was acting solely in her interest. Some fifteen minutes later Janet returned, smiled at the two men, and sat down. A man passed the compartment, and as he did so shook his head.

"How's the writing progressing?" asked Janet. She spoke in English.

"You realize you're being watched? And that all your bags have been searched," said Verrell with a smile on his face. "Incidentally, he doesn't speak English."

"I thought that apish-looking man was trying to get fresh. I didn't realize he was tailing me." Her voice was unworried. Not for the first time, he admired her courage. He knew of no one he would rather have by his side in a tough spot. Added to which she was an exceptionally charming and delightful young woman. "What's all the fuss about?"

"They're looking for the opal ring."

"What makes them think that I've got anything to do with it? If they're tailing every woman who was there last night they must be having a hell of a time!"

"Only those who wore a dark green gown."

For the first time she looked away. From where he sat, Verrell could see that she was nibbling her lips. He turned to the inspector, who had been watching them.

"Mademoiselle Dove was inquiring about my books. I'm a writer, and apparently she has read one or two of them."

The inspector grunted. "Has she said anything about last night?" he whispered behind a raised newspaper.

"Not a thing."

"On no account bring the subject up. I want to think."

"What's wrong with him?" asked Janet.

"Asking me whether you had mentioned the ring."

"He really thinks I've got it then. At least you can't be so silly. You're the only person I know who could open the safe that frightful woman keeps her jewellery in. She showed it to me once. Come to that, I suppose it wasn't you after all?"

"I only got as far as opening the door leading to the safe."

"So it was you " She stopped suddenly. Then, seeing his laughter, "All right, so I've got that ring. And what's more, I intend to keep it."

"Even when they search your person at the customs?"

For a second her eyes wavered. "Yes," she snapped.

There was silence in the carriage. Each of the occupants deep in thought. Verrell was wondering where Janet had hidden the ring. She seemed to be confident that even a search of her person would not bring it to light. In that case it could not be concealed in her clothes, since they would be rigorously examined. The same went for the heels of her shoes. Then he had an idea.

"You know, Janet, I think I preferred you when your hair was black — I can't say I like blondes."

Her eyes narrowed. "Thank goodness your likes and dislikes are no concern of mine." Deliberately she picked up a paper and began to read.

The detective asked a question, which Verrell answered, though his mind was elsewhere.

The train stopped at a station, and Verrell sent off the wire as agreed. When they moved off again he consulted his watch. In half an hour it would be time for lunch. He stood up and raised his arms as though to stretch. At that moment he lost his balance and half fell against Janet, his body between her and the inspector. His right hand, in an effort to steady himself, came up against her head, almost disarranging the large curl at the back. A moment later he straightened himself and apologized.

"Richard! If you don't give me that back I'll — "

"Not too loud. The inspector doesn't understand English — but if you make too much fuss I think he'll begin to put two and two together, Janet, *dear*."

"You swine!" she whispered, her eyes blazing. A moment later she regained her self-control.

"Are you all right?" asked the inspector.

"Yes thanks," he replied with a smile. With that he left the carriage. In his right hand, now in his pocket, rested the opal ring.

27

After two days in England, Verrell had settled back into routine. A late breakfast, late that was by an office workers standards, then the rest of the morning writing. Lunch served by Roberts, his valet, followed by another three hours' work. After that he spent his time as the whim took him.

The third day he decided, for once, to break routine and to visit the neighbourhood of the club mentioned in Janet's letter. As a companion she was all that any man could hope for, and her tastes were similar to his. So similar that they had first met over a safe! And he wanted to see her again, for her own sake. Further, that letter had roused his curiosity. It was so curt and so oddly phrased that he scented a mystery; and a mystery to Blackshirt was as undeclared income to a tax inspector. What arrangement was to be arranged; and why the insistence on no funny tricks 'this' time? Also the fact that the letter had been unsigned left Verrell in a restless mood eager to solve the riddle.

He soon found Wells Street, which led off Oxford Street, and parked his car half-way along. The telephone directory had listed the number as 355, so, finding he was opposite number 277, he walked briskly along the pavement. London fascinated him. The never-ending scurry for wealth, happiness, success, each person with nose to the grindstone slaving away, for what? If they obtained what they had set out to do they were not content. They wanted more. What was the secret behind this never-ending bustle? Then there was the other side of London. The side he had known in childhood, and from which he had dragged himself by hard work and nimble fingers. Where one in two of the men had been in prison, or would be before they died, and where wives and children were beaten when the men came home drunk. It still made him shudder to remember his foster-parents. Brutal, without a spark of decency, they had forced him into a life of crime. Small, petty offences at first; then his superior intelligence, inherited from the parents he would never know, increased his skill until he was the master and they the pupils. They were killed. War came and Verrell, as he now called himself, had volunteered. Later he began to write, and had made sufficient to be able to retire from his life of crime — but he hadn't, because the lure, the challenge of danger was too great.

With a start Verrell realized he had walked past the number he required. He retraced his steps; 355 was a two-storey building. Inside was a small hall, with the names of various firms on brass plates. The Locano Club was on the basement level. A small door led into a passageway at the end of which was a desk, with a typist busy at her machine. It was some moments before she attended him.

"Yes, sir?"

"Can you tell me, please, at what hours the club is open."

"From ten to four. Drinks must be off the table at two," she said in a bored voice.

"Does one have to be a member?"

"Yes, sir. You must be proposed by an existing member, seconded by another."

"That's a nuisance. I'm afraid I don't know any members, but a friend of mine who came here as a guest especially recommended it." He smiled. His face held considerable charm and the typist was impressed.

"I'll just speak to Mr. Clayton, sir, and see if he can help you."

She was gone a short while, then returned with a man whose black hair was swept back and plastered down with grease, and who sported a loud and offensive tie.

"Miss Phibbs informs me you wish to become a member, but do not know anyone here."

"That's correct."

"I'm afraid, sir, there's not much we can do. The regulations are strict. But what is your name, please?"

"Verrell. Richard Verrell."

"Not the author?"

"Yes."

The man's manner thawed. "In that case, sir, I'm certain we can arrange matters. If you will pay the three guineas subscription I will see that everything is in order. May I book you a table?"

"Yes, if you would. I shall be along tonight."

"For how many?"

"Two. I shall arrange to meet someone here."

"Very good, sir."

Verrell left the building, a member of the club.

*

Since the Locano Club was not far from his flat, Verrell chose to walk. His was an athletic nature, and, unlike the majority of the inhabitants of London, he did not seek the quickest form of conveyance to get from A to B. Briskly he strode along the pavements. His visit tonight was in the nature of a skirmish. He might, or might not, meet Janet there, together with the writer of the note, but should he decide to visit the club at some 'unusual' hour, he would know the lie of the land.

The dance floor was in the shape of an L, with the band at the turn. Lights were so low that waiters had to use pocket-torches to illuminate the wine lists, where everything cost twice as much as it was worth... it was in no way different from a dozen other such places. Even those present had the same jaded, hot house look as their counterparts.

There were four doors in all, not counting the entrance. Two led to the cloak-rooms; one was used by the waiters; while the other had so far opened only once to admit a man in evening dress; from his actions Verrell judged him to be the manager. If there were any rooms connected with the club where he might expect to find Janet, the fourth door offered the only reasonable access. Since there was no time like the present, he decided to investigate that exit.

His chance came when the lights were even further dimmed and the cabaret show commenced. Verrell rose from the table and walked in the direction of the cloak-room. The chorus, now high-stepping on the dance floor, had entered by that same fourth door, which lay some three yards from where he now stood. So far as he could see, no one was watching him, so with a confident stride he passed through the swinging door. Before him was another door on the right, then stairs leading up to a landing. From his right he could hear the high chatter of women, so, pausing an instant to see whether his departure from the room had been noticed, he went up. The landing led into a small passageway which ended at a window. There was one door on either side of the passage, and one where he was standing. He could hear nothing from that room, so he walked noiselessly along until he could listen at the door to his right. From inside came the murmur of voices. A man's voice rose sufficiently for Verrell to distinguish what he was saying, and also to identify the speaker. He started — then laughed. For it was none other than Peebles, alias the Jackdaw.

"By all the saints!" he chuckled. Though it seemed incredible, Peebles must have written the letter, offering, presumably, to give Janet a job. No need to ask what kind of job! If Blackshirt were the cleverest cracksman in the country, the Jackdaw ran him a close second!

He gripped the door-knob with his right hand and very gently moved it. When he had turned it to its full limit he pushed. The door opened a fraction. Sufficient for him to distinguish everything that was said.

"I tell you I don't like it, Peebles. Damned if I do! You know what happened last time — who's to say the bi—"

"Shut up, Jim. And this goes for you others. I'm in charge of things. If you don't like the way I handle them — then get out, right now." There was a harsh note in his voice. Ostensibly a retired colonial, behind his mask of an easy-going affluent man, there was a savage streak. "Just get this into your thick skulls. This time we'll have the goods, so if she wants to play funny then she'll be left twiddling her thumbs. But Janet will be a bit too careful looking after her own interests to think of double-crossing us again. She'll want paying as much as you will, and it just won't be any use her cutting up funny because if she does..." He left the rest of the sentence unspoken, but Verrell could imagine his shrugging his broad shoulders.

"Surely, Jim, you don't think I'd let you all down? After we've all worked together. Besides, as Peebles says, I need the money."

There was a muttering, unintelligible, which Verrell guessed was Jim's.

"Damned if I know how you managed to spend so much," said Peebles in a surly tone. "They'd have kept us going for years. Trust a woman to spend the stuff like water." Evidently the incident still rankled.

There was a pause. Then, "Now let's get down to business, Janet, you'll go down and apply for this position. If the housekeeper likes you, then the old girl'll have you. Jim's seen that the housekeeper's squared. Haven't you, Jim?"

"Yep. Told the old bag she was my niece, what wanted a good position as governess. That and a few quid soon made certain."

"Janet will be in the house. Jim, you'll stay at the pub close by and study the district, until you know every lane. Harry and me will be up here getting everything ready, we'll come down on the evening of the fifth. The twenty-first birthday is three days later; the big dance they're attending is on the third. So it's odds on that they'll keep the pearls out of the bank for those four days anyway. Janet will be able to let us know about that; also a plan of the house. Once we get our hands on the Darthweight pearls we'll be sitting pretty for a long while. But God help any of you if you bungle things!"

Blackshirt's eyes sparkled. The Darthweight pearls — one of the finest collections in the world, unmatched for their perfect shape and colouring. Collected by countless generations of Darthweights. So the Jackdaw was making a bid for them — well, there'd be someone else bidding, with a higher limit!

Just then a gun pressed hard into his back. "Shove your hands above your head, mister, and walk inside."

Blackshirt cursed. He had been so engrossed in what was happening inside that he had been caught off balance.

Slowly he raised his hands, poised ready to take advantage of the slightest chance to escape.

The man felt his tension. He dug the gun harder into Blackshirt's back.

There was nothing to do but enter. He walked into the room.

Peebles glanced up, annoyed at the interruption. "Blackshirt!" he cried out in shocked surprise.

Chapter Four

The others present were equally surprised. Behind him Blackshirt heard the man swear.

Janet was the first to recover. "You certainly get around! But this time I'm almost glad to see you." She smiled warmly.

"What do you mean, this time?" queried Peebles angrily.

"Didn't I tell you I met Richard on the train coming back from France?"

"No you damn well didn't. And I suppose that's why we have Mr. Nosey Parker here now. Look here, Janet, if you think you're going to play us for suckers again, I'll cheerfully twist your neck."

"Allow me to explain," interrupted Blackshirt easily, "I was in your club downstairs this evening — . — "

"Let's finish this perishing blighter once and for all," snarled Jim, his rage overcoming discretion.

"Quit it," snapped Peebles. He turned. "Now, just what in the hell *are* you doing here?"

"I came here this evening and a few minutes ago I had cause to leave my table. I walked through what I thought was the right door, but the only place it seemed to lead to was up here. Just as I was leaving I heard your voice and I was intending to drop in on you when your friend here pushed a gun in my back."

"What made you come to this place?"

"A friend of mine recommended it. Though I wish you'd lower the price of your drinks! "

"I suppose he just happened to tell you about it, right after you'd met Janet! Harry, what do you mean by letting him come up here?"

"I couldn't help it, Peebles. I felt so thirsty I went to get a glass of water and — "

"The last time you drank water was when you were too young to know anything else existed. How long were you away from the door?"

"I weren't more than half a minute, at the most. Honest. If this cove had time to do more than get near the door, I'll give my share of what's coming to charity!" He spoke hurriedly.

Peebles glared from one to the other. "You'd better be telling the truth or I'll see you don't drink another glass of anything!"

There was silence. Then harshly Peebles ordered the other men out of the room. When they had gone, "Just what in the hell are you doing here? If I thought you were trying to double-cross me again I'd —"

"To tell you the truth, Peebles, I came to look for Janet. As a matter of fact I found this address in her handbag. The detective in the train asked me if I knew it."

"What detective?"

"One who rather thought Janet had an opal ring with her."

"Not that ring belonging to Vanes, or some such name, who lives in the south of France."

"That's right. Janet was at the dance."

Peebles chuckled. "Still at your old game, Janet. Never thought of you when I read it had been stolen." He seemed satisfied that Blackshirt's presence was not connected with the projected theft of the Darthweight pearls — and when his own plans were not in danger, Peebles could be entirely pleasant. "Now I suppose you'll be buying some new clothes."

"No, I won't. I had it in the train — until I met Richard."

As Peebles digested the information he laughed. "Damn well wish I'd been there to see it. What happened?"

Blackshirt told him, and even Janet had to grin at the humour of the situation. "I really ought to thank you, Richard," she said, "when I got to the customs they went over me with a fine-toothed comb. If I had had it, I'm afraid they might have found it. What made them so suspicious I can't think! Anyway, let bygones be bygones. Are you going to take me out to dinner some time?"

"I'd love to, if Peebles doesn't mind. I missed you when you went away," he added sincerely.

"Not the only one," muttered Peebles feelingly.

"I must be off," said Verrell. "How will Tuesday evening suit you? A dinner-dance somewhere."

"Sounds lovely. I'll give you a ring to confirm."

He turned to go. "Just one thing," said Peebles. "Don't bother to come back here. The manager will have instructions to prevent your entry. And in case you still think of poking your nose where it's not wanted, I'll give Harry instructions to deal with you without referring to me. And for your information the boys are still sore — sore enough to get tough! "

"Good night," replied Verrell pleasantly, as though he had not heard the last few words.

Peebles glared at the door. Blackshirt did not appear to have heard anything — but he knew to his cost just how rapidly the other could work.

As Verrell walked home he gaily hummed a tune. The Jackdaw had ordered him to keep off — the surest way to invite him in on whatever was doing. If things worked out the way he thought they might, then the Jackdaw would find the safe empty!

Some two years ago, he had considered securing the pearls and had visited the district, but a scrap of information had prevented his continuing with the idea. The Darthweight family practically always kept the jewels in the local bank — and that was one place Blackshirt was not prepared to tackle! But he now knew that they would be at the house for four or five days, and further that the Jackdaw intended to steal them on the fifth. If the dance was on the third, then on the night of the fourth they would be lying in the safe. It was on that night that he must go into action!

Even as he was walking along the road his mind was inventing and discarding possibilities.

The following morning he worked on his new novel. The idea had come to him while abroad, and the first half was clearly mapped out in his mind. After three hours' work he pushed the manuscript to one side, and drew forward the luncheon-tray which Roberts had prepared. Discarding all thoughts of the novel, he tackled the delicious chicken salad and concentrated on an even more engrossing subject.

The little he knew of Lodestone Manor, the home of the Darthweights, was certainly not favourable from his point of view. During his previous casual tour of the immediate neighbourhood, he had seen how well the place was guarded. Generally, before attempting any job, Verrell spent days in meticulous survey of the house in question. Every means of entry and exit; known hazards such as night guards, watchdogs; or possibilities of danger such as burglar alarms. Casual discussions with the locals over a pint of beer often elicited useful information; a careful survey of the house itself, through a pair of high-power binoculars, frequently proved worthwhile. To such painstaking research, and the fact that he usually gave up the idea if the job proved more than even he cared to tackle, he owed his continued liberty.

Lodestone Manor could be said to be neither impregnable, nor an easy task. To begin with, a high wall right round the house provided the first difficulty, but one that could be fairly easily overcome since a large part of it was well beyond the reflection of any light. The two gates were watched rather than guarded by gatekeepers who, as far as Verrell knew, slept at night. But to offset these advantages was the fact that according to the locals — and confirmed by one of the gamekeepers in a heated discussion on partridge shooting — the lower windows were all guarded by burglar alarms of some patent manufacture which guaranteed that the wires could not be cut.

Access to the second floor could be obtained by way of the bathroom at the rear of the house, the windows of which might be reached from a handy drain-pipe. The trouble was the size of the window; Verrell had doubts as to whether even his slim body could squeeze through. This means of entry was, however, the only practicable one, since the second floor was high enough to necessitate a ladder too large for one man to handle alone.

Once before he had broken into a tool-shed, removed a large and clumsy ladder, tried to prop it against a window, missed the balance — and had had to run hell for leather as splitting glass roused the entire household.

Again, the whereabouts of the safe was a matter of conjecture — as also the safe itself. More times than he cared to remember, Blackshirt had broken into a house after meticulous planning, only to find himself faced with a safe that was beyond his skill.

Even as he weighed the pros and cons he knew, come what may, he would make the attempt. A carefree smile softened his features as he finished the last mouthful of chicken and waited for Roberts to serve the sweet.

After lunch he decided to take a break from work and go for a walk. Along Oxford Street he paused before a large notice which advertised a display, in the building behind, of many famous and priceless jewels. According to the text of the advertisement, no one could fail to be thrilled by such a wealth of jewels, many worth a king's ransom. Unable to believe that the owners of the jewels would risk their being displayed to the public in such surroundings, he examined the notice at closer quarters — and chuckled when he read, in very small type, the statement that the display was composed of replicas, indistinguishable from the originals. Admission was sixpence. He paid and entered, though not without a feeling that he was throwing away the money: he had an instinctive aversion to anything shoddy.

The 'collection' was housed in glass cases ranged along three sides of a moderately deep room which had, until recently, been used as an amusement arcade. Another glass case occupied the centre of the floor. In spite of being jostled bv a crowd of school-children, who gazed in rapt awe and admiration at the exhibits, he smiled as he passed round the room. Jewels worth a king's ransom! If they had been real, not even an Indian potentate could have produced one quarter of their value. The famous Turnstone diamonds were there, so large it seemed impossible that they could be true to scale. The Phillip rubies, second only to the Rosalea set — still causing headaches because of their disappearance — and many others.

Presently he moved to the centre case, which contained only pearls — and there he saw the Darthweight pearls, resting in a nest of black velvet. The sight of them suggested the germ of an idea which set his blood racing. He laughed joyfully — much to the amazement of the children who surrounded him.

*

As the grandmother clock chimed the hour of s a.m., Richard Verrell closed the novel he had been reading. He lit a cigarette, moved into his bedroom, carefully drew the curtains, and opened the wardrobe door. This solid but cleverly constructed piece of furniture was dusted by Roberts each morning — but there was one part of it that Roberts never handled. At the touch of a hidden spring, the false back slid open to reveal the small space in which Blackshirt kept his 'working clothes'.

Having stripped to the skin he first buckled round his waist the belt which held his complete set of tools. After special underclothing which lacked any means of identification, he donned the famous black shirt which had gained him his nickname; then dress trousers and jacket, black nylon socks and black patent leather shoes. Round his neck he wound a white scarf which quickly and effectively hid the black shirt beneath. Over all he wore a light-weight raincoat made so that it would slip into his pocket. Next, he folded a black nylon hood which he put into his right-hand trouser-pocket. Lastly, he set a tall hat at a jaunty angle on his head... to all intents Blackshirt was a man about town in evening dress, returning from a night out! Yet, with one movement it was possible to strip off the white scarf, adjust the hood, and become no more than a black shadow, practically invisible at night.

His method of leaving his flat was unorthodox but practical. One reason for having chosen the flat was that the back windows overlooked a small courtyard belonging to a day garage, which closed promptly at 10.30 each evening. The courtyard was completely hidden from the rest of the world so that Blackshirt was able to climb out of the window and shin down a convenient drain-pipe. At the entrance to the courtyard he paused and glanced quickly up and down the street. There was no one in sight. A moment later Blackshirt was walking unconcernedly along the road in the direction of Oxford Street.

For once he was uncertain of his next move. Judging by the intrinsic value of the collection, Blackshirt was certain that the display was unlikely to be guarded. The street door, of course, would be barred in the usual manner, and entry would have to be made from the side.

Upon reaching the corner of the side-street Blackshirt paused for a moment to glance down the road. Observing that it was empty he turned into it, and approached the entrance to the offices above the collection. A glance at the lock assured him that he should encounter no difficulties. With a quick movement he inserted a small steel instrument into the keyhole. One turn, and the bolt moved back. He slipped inside, removed his scarf and adjusted his hood.

Standing still, he waited a few minutes to make sure that his entry had been unobserved. Only a faint squeal indicated the presence of anything living… mice. At last, satisfied that he had not been seen, he re-locked the outside door although, in the event of an emergency, his way out was blocked. On the other hand, he preferred not to take the risk of having an inquiring constable push it open. Again he waited to see if the slight sound had disturbed anyone before he made his next move.

All remained quiet, so he adjusted the patent shutter of his electric torch which reduced the beam of light to a pinpoint. Before him was a long corridor with a staircase at the end. Silently he advanced, altering his balance with each step so that, should he find a board that squealed, he could throw his weight backwards in time to prevent too much noise.

Maintaining the utmost caution he ascended the first twelve stairs to a half-landing. Here the staircase took a turn to the right, but after half a dozen more stairs he reached the first floor. At this point he switched off his torch, for fear that a night-watchman was somewhere in the building. Using his outstretched arms and his sensitive finger-tips as eyes he moved slowly along the passage which led to the offices. At the end was a window overlooking the street. Having made quite certain that the curtains were well drawn, he risked another flash with the torch. He then carefully paced the floor until he arrived opposite a door which he judged belonged to a room immediately over the showroom. According to the wording on the glass panel, it was used by a firm of chartered accountants. After the usual precautionary pause he started on the job of opening the door, by oiling the hinges to deaden any noise they might make.

The office was large, with two desks against opposite walls which were lined with book-cases and filing cabinets.

Blackshirt knelt down and inspected the floor. It was old, and not in good condition, but even so it was going to be a hard tussle to break through it. Choosing a spot within the shadow of the farthest desk, Blackshirt took off the belt of tools and unrolled it. He selected a brace and bit and then rapidly drilled a series of holes in the form of a square. Then with a keyhole-saw he commenced the arduous task of cutting through the boards. Halfway round he paused and removed the hood, wiped the sweat from his brow with a handkerchief. Ruefully he considered the trouble he was going to, merely to obtain something that was probably worth less than the entrance money. Replacing the hood he resumed work, and after another half hour was able to remove the square. Beneath him, a foot below the level he was on, was the lath and plaster ceiling of the room. He slid the board between the two floors, replaced his tools around his waist, and then unwound a hank of thin, wire-cored rope. This he secured to the desk, then knotted it at three-foot intervals.

The ceiling was easy to pierce, but Blackshirt had to be careful that too large a lump did not fall below and break one of the showcases — with attendant noise — but he managed it without alarm, and lowered himself below.

The showcase was padlocked, but the flat glass top was thin, and quickly Blackshirt cut out a circle and withdrew the 'pearls'. He was on the point of climbing upwards when faintly from above came the sound of men's voices.

"Look 'ere, Bert, I saw a ruddy light, and that's that! I went across to Sammy's stall to get a cup of tea, and when I came back I saw a perishin' flash through the end winder."

"More like you been seeing things. Bottle of something you've tucked away," replied a second voice in surly tones. "Waste of time, I call it, coming up 'ere just because you've been seeing things. The ruddy sergeant'll be along any moment now, and if I'm not there to meet him he'll want to know what's what."

"Ain't you paid to apre'end the criminals?"

"You look after your business and I'll look after mine. If I've come looking for lights in this 'ere building once, I've done it a dozen times.

And every time, what do we find? You've been seein' things. And last time the sarge threatened to log me if he found me in this building once more! And heaven only knows why I'm 'ere now!"

The footsteps were approaching. At any moment the men would be in the room directly above. From an indistinct mumble, Blackshirt was able to distinguish every word.

"Now then, Joe, which of these rooms did you think you saw a light just now? Soon as we find it's all clear I can return."

"This one 'ere. Them chartered accountants have it."

A blaze of light reached down through the ceiling as the light was switched on.

"There we are. Empty as usual! Not surprised with all these dusty old papers about. Not what I'd call a good crib; unless your burglar friend's going in for waste paper." The policeman laughed.

The first man walked farther into the room. Suddenly his gaze became fixed at a spot beyond the far desk. "All right — so I'm seeing things. Then what's that ruddy big hole doing in the floor?"

The constable acted quickly. "'Ere, you're right! Drat this torch, never does work properly... that's better... now then, hang on to me middle." He bent down, and with the other's help directed the light round the showroom. It appeared to be empty. "I'm going down, see what's what. Though what anyone hopes to get from there beats me. Here, grab me torch a minute."

The constable lowered himself through the hole in the floor, grunting with the effort, then, clutching hold of the rope with one arm, retrieved the light from the worried watchman.

"Take this whistle, Joe, and if I shout, blow as hard as you know how. That'll bring the sarge along — I left the door open below."

The constable descended two feet until he was clear of the ceiling of the room below. Clutching heroically to the swinging rope he shone his light around the room. Save for the various showcases, the room still appeared empty.

Joe, above, was not feeling at peace with the world. In the first place, although the rope led down below, he had first seen the flash from the level he was on himself. Therefore, it seemed to his somewhat nervous mind that the intruder was just as likely to have remained on the first floor as to be down below. The policeman was paid to apprehend law-breakers and endure the possibility of attack while so doing, but he felt that his small salary was more than earned by merely patrolling the corridors. Should the unknown be on his level it was logical to foresee a strong possibility that he might suffer harm of a violent nature — Joe kept the police whistle in hand, ready to send out a loud and insistent blast at the slightest need.

From below came the hollow echo of a dull thud. Joe's heart began to pitter-patter as his imagination worked at top speed. He gulped.

"Are you all right, Bert?" he called down in a timid whisper.

"Shut up, and keep an eye open up top." If Bert's voice was brusque it was with good reason: he had misjudged the distance. True, he had sat down on that part of him normally reserved for sitting, but with rather more force than was usual.

Joe kept an eye open; in fact, he turned at frequent intervals to make sure that no one was creeping up on him with malice aforethought. Presently he heard the sound of another crash from below, which was followed by a low grunt. But this time he thought he had better remain silent; the constable, it seemed, was inclined to be touchy.

He complimented himself on his discretion three minutes later, when the policeman's helmet began to rise up through the hole in the floor. Evidently everything was in order below…

Then, "Slip your arms under me armpits, Joe, then grip your hands together and hold on."

Joe was one of the simple, obedient kind. It was not for him to wonder why. He kneeled down on the floor beside the hole, slipped his hands under the constable's arms, and, as directed, held tight. No sooner had he done so than he felt the whole weight of the other man trying to pull him down. He began to puff and grunt in his tremendous effort to hold up the heavy policeman.

Then an amazing thing happened — another head came into sight through the hole, a head entirely concealed in a black hood. But this head was quickly followed by a slim, lithe pair of shoulders, clad in a black shirt. Before Joe could recover his stupefied amazement the black-garbed body had somehow slithered its way through the hole past Joe's motionless head, and was standing beside him, patting his shoulder in a friendly way.

"Don't let go whatever you do, Joe, old boy. It's a long way to fall, and Bert wouldn't thank you to drop him. Cheerio. Give my love to Bert when he comes round…"

Long after Blackshirt had left the vicinity Joe was still in the same position. He knew it was his duty to chase the intruder, or at least do something more active, but he hadn't the strength to pull Bert up higher, and he daren't let go. And Joe didn't think Bert would care for being dropped. Not one bit...

Chapter Five

Two days later, the phone rang as Verrell was about to sit down to lunch. He lifted the receiver.

"Verrell speaking."

"Richard, Janet here."

"Hallo, Janet, about time you phoned, I was beginning to think you'd stood me down."

"I've been terribly busy and this is the first chance I've had to get in touch with you. Is that dinner invite still going?"

"Of course."

"Will tonight suit you? I'm afraid it's the only time I can manage as I'm going into the country for a few days tomorrow."

"Fine. How about eight-thirty at the Chrysler. Or I'll pick you up wherever you're staying."

"Make it there."

Shortly afterwards she ran off and Verrell called out to his valet, "Roberts, put my dress suit out, will you, I'll be going out tonight."

"Very good, sir."

During lunch he found himself looking forward to the evening. Whatever Janet might be — and was, with interest — she was one of the most charming women he knew. There had always been a bond between them of something more than friendship, and something less than love. Perhaps, a semi-permanent flirtation expressed it best. He admired her nerve and courage, and she in turn recognized that though he might step across the boundaries that hemmed in the law-abiding citizen, at heart he was an anomaly — since he was honest.

Janet could see from Verrell's eyes that the time she had spent dressing had not been wasted. She was looking extraordinarily vivacious and pretty in a black and gold strapless evening dress with a small fur cape over her shoulders. Her hair had resumed its normal colour, and she had had it cut short in the prevailing fashion. It brought out her impish character.

"Come and have a drink before we sit down," he suggested, linking his arm in hers and walking towards the small bar just beyond the entrance to the ballroom.

"Yes, sir," said the bartender.

"Two Martinis," ordered Verrell, remembering Janet's favourite cocktail.

"Success to all our ventures," he toasted. When they had finished, the head waiter showed them to a corner seat, sufficiently far from the band not to be drowned in a torrent of noise.

After ordering they joined in the dancing.

"Happy?" asked Janet, as they waltzed round the not too crowded floor.

"Very. And you?"

"I always am, with you," she replied sincerely. "You're one of the few men I like and can trust. Besides, you're a very good dancer."

Just then the music ceased and the orchestra rose in order to make way for a 'South American' band. Never having fully understood the intricacies of the mamba, Verrell suggested they return to their table.

"I'm glad to be back," said Janet with a sigh. "It may be an exceedingly dull and worthy place, but there's something about England that one can't find anywhere else. Maybe it's our 'wonderful policemen'," she said with a laugh.

"Tell me, Janet, have you spent everything you made from the rubies? I expected you to be set for life. You really ought to have been there to see Peebles's face. I thought he'd have a fit!"

"Probably just as well I wasn't. I don't think he finds it quite so amusing as you do. Yes, I am as broke as broke can be. Somebody introduced me to roulette and before I knew what had happened there wasn't enough to pay the hotel bill. That's why I was up at Varnes's that night — though a fat lot of good it did me! "

"If I could lend you something, Janet' until "

"Thanks a lot, but — no." She laid her hand on his arm. "But I've got something that might interest you. You know I'm with Peebles at the moment?"

"Yes."

"Before I went there I heard of some jewels that would make even you sit up. And in the past few days I've managed to get hold of some information that might interest you." She paused as the waiter came forward and served the first course.

Verrell's face remained non-committal. It seemed as if she were going to outline the scheme that he had heard only a few days before — but then it had not included Blackshirt. Was it possible that she was seeking his aid to pick the fruit of the Jackdaw's labour once again? Not for the first time he was amazed that she had such an open and engaging face. If he were right in his conjecture, then she…

"A penny for them."

"Nothing really. I was thinking of a film I saw last week."

"Oh!" She sounded disappointed. "Then you weren't considering what I have just said?"

"You didn't say anything for me to consider."

"Beast," she replied. Then she leaned slightly forward. "Richard, have you heard of the Darthweight pearls?" "Vaguely."

"Don't be so irritating, you must have heard of them. They're one of the most famous sets in England. If you won't listen I'll not say another word."

"Will you have some more wine?" asked Verrell blandly.

"Be quiet, Richard. Suppose I told you that the pearls will be at Lodestone Manor for a few days, because of a dance and birthday party? Would that make you interested?"

He started as she had hoped he would. But in his case it was sheer amazement. So she was intending to double-cross the Jackdaw; as calmly as that!

"Are you suggesting I?"

"I'm not suggesting anything until I've finished. Tomorrow I'm joining the family as governess to two little brats they've got."

"Heaven help them!"

"There's just under a week before the pearls are brought into the house and in that time, with any luck, I'll be able to get a good idea of the layout of the house, and the routine of the family. Peeb — I've heard that safe is pretty old-fashioned and more than I could tackle, but equally certainly a cinch for you. Now do you understand what I'm getting at?"

"Who gave you this idea, Janet?"

"No one. But I need the money, and when I heard that the pearls were staying in the house for a few days I thought it was a natural."

"You've already got the job as governess?"

"Yes. Start tomorrow at a salary of just over six pounds a week — plus keep, of course."

"It's a wonder the Jackdaw didn't think along the same lines. I suppose this isn't his idea?" he asked innocently.

"He's much too busy at the moment, otherwise he might have done. Besides, you don't think I'd do a trick like that, surely?" she asked with hurt expression.

Verrell mumbled something.

"If you're agreeable I thought the evening of the fourth might be O.K. The family will have the pearls in the safe then, and it will give me time to let you know how things stand."

Unless his memory was failing, thought Verrell, that was the day before the Jackdaw had arranged. "Suppose I do as you suggest, what will you do?"

"I'll leave the house with you — when you've got the pearls. That would probably be safer than remaining on."

A lot safer, he thought, in the light of who was due the next evening 1 His eyes twinkled as he thought of the probable consequences. Janet was watching closely and she breathed a small sigh.

"How about it, Richard?"

"If I say no, will you still go down there as governess?"

"Of course."

"I don't believe you. You'd worked out the whole plan with me in mind — and now you're trying to tell me this. Confess."

"As a matter of fact you're right, Richard dear, but I knew you'd fall for anything that offered some excitement!"

There was silence as each digested what had passed. They were both satisfied. Then, dismissing the subject they relaxed and enjoyed themselves.

When he returned to his flat that night, Verrell was certain of one thing — Janet had the most adorable pair of lips.

*

On the Saturday, Richard Verrell motored down into the heart of the weald of Kent; where, at a convenient side-turning remembered from a previous visit, he parked his car. Presently he walked along the road for some fifty yards or so, then, turning right, he entered a small wood.

At the edge of the wood he sat down, and having adjusted his binoculars he surveyed the scene before him. The wood was on a slight rise which overlooked Lodestone Manor, so from where he sat he had a perfectly clear view of the back of the house. So far as he could judge nothing had changed since his previous visit. The lawns were as well tended; as were the hedges of clipped box. A gravel path was very much in evidence, so he registered a reminder to bring two strips of felt.

For the moment he concentrated on a small window he had noted before, which could be reached by way of a drainpipe that ran straight down the side of the house. The point which had to be settled was whether the window was large enough for him to wriggle through. He decided that it would just about allow his slim body to manoeuvre, but probably only with a tight squeeze. So much so that he did not overlook the possibility of his finding himself stuck half-way…

For the next two hours he studied the approach to the house in minute detail, occasionally making cryptic notes in a small pocket-book. Satisfied, at length, that he could learn no more, he returned to his car and drove off, whistling cheerfully.

Four days later Janet phoned as she had promised, from a small village near Lodestone Manor. In guarded language she gave him a rough description of the household, its ways and difficulties.

She went on to suggest the small window of the back bathroom as being the only feasible means of entry; and promised to send a plan of the house at once, together with the time and place of an appointment for Tuesday night. The safe, she said, was in the library; behind a false book-case which was wired to an alarm. She was not quite sure how the false book-case was operated, but believed by a simple spring action, set in motion from the left-hand side of the case. Before ringing off she murmured a few words that made her listener's eyes glint, and a dreamy smile soften his face.

That night he spent two hours in concentrated thought, smoking innumerable cigarettes, before he finally perfected his plan. When at last he turned in he did so with a gay heart.

*

Janet's letter arrived on the morning of the fourth. Blackshirt noted with satisfaction that, as might have been expected from so thorough a worker, it was detailed to the last obstacle — even the bathroom window had been measured. There was a lot to be said, he thought, for working with someone else — that is if the other person could be trusted! — even though his amazing success in avoiding the clutches of the law was almost certainly due to his working alone.

Accompanying the plan was a short note. The household was a methodical one. At ten-thirty the family retired, the servants then locked up. By eleven-thirty everybody was in bed; and by twelve, during the nights she had so far been there, the house was completely quiet. She could promise to be waiting at 2.30 a.m. inside the bathroom, from which point they could proceed to the library.

He first memorized the plan, and then carefully burnt it, together with the letter. He still had several hours to while away before indulging in his own little scheme, a quixotic one, possibly, but one dear to his nature.

At ten-thirty he went to his bedroom, opened the recess in his cupboard, and took out the famous suit of clothes. In ten minutes he was dressed in the latest fashion of a 'man about town'; the white scarf tied neatly round his neck to conceal the black shirt; his black hat set at a jaunty angle on his head. From a drawer he extracted two narrow strips of felt which, tightly rolled, fitted into his coat pockets. With a last quick check to see that he had everything he let himself out of the front door, and strode smartly along the pavement towards a side-street where drivers were in the habit of parking cars for some hours. He picked a fast, inconspicuous model and drove off.

Owing to clear roads and favourable traffic lights, he was able to park the car alongside the woods by a quarter to twelve, having carefully reversed it into a convenient spot where it was concealed by an overhanging tree and thick undergrowth. Then he took off the coat — after withdrawing the two rolls of felt — and left it on the back seat, together with his white scarf and hat. Should he have to abandon them there was nothing by which he could be traced. He took off the brown leather gloves, bought that afternoon from a multiple stores, and drew on a pair of black nylon, which covered his hands while leaving them supple enough for the intricate work which lay ahead. He adjusted his hood, and became a shadow which merged so completely with the dark night that only a direct beam of light would reveal his presence. One last thing remained to be done. From the side-pocket of the car he withdrew a leather bag which contained the 'pearls' he had gone to so much trouble to obtain.

The hill was not steep, but the woods provided an obstacle that necessitated the use of his sense of touch. Long practice had enabled him to use arms and legs as an extra 'eye' at night-time. Advancing slowly, and holding his arms before him to give warning of trees, he cleared the strip of wood in less than fifteen minutes, with a minimum of noise.

The hill gave way to flat pasture land, which in turn led to the wall surrounding Lodestone Manor. Age had worn the surface and left sufficient holds for the athletic Blackshirt to scramble over. Having dropped down on the far side he waited for a while, listening to see whether his entry had been detected. But nothing, beyond the normal night-life of the country, was to be heard.

From the direction in which he was approaching the house, there was first a vegetable garden, then an area of lawn bordered by a gravel path. Before crossing this he reconnoitred the immediate grounds. So far as he could see, the house was in darkness; but he could not afford to take chances since it was relatively early in the morning. He encircled the manor, secure in the knowledge that even had anyone been looking, they could have seen nothing. He arrived back at his starting-point without having seen a light anywhere.

He then unrolled the two pieces of felt which he tied to the soles of his shoes. He placed one foot on the gravel and then gradually transferred his weight from the other foot — there was not a sound. Very slowly he repeated the operation. In this manner he crossed the path and came against the wall of the house, directly by the drain-pipe.

Raising his hands above his head, he gripped the pipe with them, dug his toes into the angle between it and the wall, then gripped the pipe with his knees and carefully raised himself so that he could take another grip with his hands, a few inches higher. It was no easy task, but because of his fine physical condition and constant practice he safely reached the level of the window-sill on which he presently rested precariously, while he used his free hand to reach into his shirt and extract a long steel tool from his belt. Inserted between the two sashes and moved sharply to one side, it quickly released the catch.

Inch by inch he raised the lower half of the window, pausing whenever it made the faintest of protesting squeaks. As soon as there was enough room he eased his body in until he found a solid foundation on which to rest his feet, which later proved to be the rim of the bath. With a carefree smile he noted that an extra inch to his hips would have been just too bad...

There was a conglomeration of sounds so slight that they could have been heard only by a pair of keen ears. A whisper from behind him was really the creaking of a window-frame due to nothing in particular save, possibly, the old house turning round in its sleep. A quick patter from overhead denoted marauding mice; but a creak from outside the door made him poise himself in readiness for danger. When it was not repeated he relaxed — an old building at night was no place for the faint-hearted!

49

He opened the bathroom door, having oiled the hinges in case they should squeal, and peered into the darkness ahead. Every nerve in his body responded to the thrill of danger; every muscle was braced for instant action should it become necessary.

Janet's directions had shown a passage of some twenty yards connecting the bathroom with the main building; opening into this passage were the staff bedrooms. At the farther end he would have to turn right and walk along a carpeted floor until he came to the gun-room, which led directly to the library.

Had anyone been posted along the route that Blackshirt took, with knowledge of his intended movements, the watcher would still have been unaware of the cracksman's passing — so silent was he. It was not until he entered the library that he used his specially shuttered torch. Adjusting it so that only a pin-prick of light was visible, he flashed it over the room. Three walls were covered by book-shelves; the fourth, broken by two bay windows, had a desk against the wall. Heavy brocade curtains were drawn across the windows and two doors — evidently the owner appreciated warmth and had been determined to shut out all draught. Having checked the curtains to make sure there was no possibility of a glimmer of light escaping, he switched on the small electric light over the book-shelves built against the east wall.

Part of the book-case was false — but the question was which part? Examining it inch by inch he presently discovered what he had been searching for — a small break in the woodwork extending from top to bottom, four feet from one end. Direct leverage having had no effect he began to remove some of the books, deeming that the most probable hiding-place of the spring. At the back of the third shelf he discovered a small keyhole.

Unusual, he mused, to lock the 'secret' hiding-place — usually it worked on a spring. He stepped back and inspected the shelves with a searching gaze. Presently he noticed a pair of electric wires that led from the ceiling to that part of the book-case. Cunning, he thought. With the help of a pair of insulated wire-cutters he first cut the two wires, and then tried the lock with a series of skeleton keys. Upon turning the third key the tumblers clicked, and the case swung open to reveal a safe of strong but old design.

Turning the dial was painstaking work that necessitated endless patience, incredibly keen fingers, and good hearing. Back and forth he turned it, keeping an even, patient tempo which took no account of time... in spite of the fact that he had set himself a time-table that had to be strictly adhered to. But at last he heard the faint welcome 'click' and, with a turn of the handle, opened the safe.

Inside was a mass of papers, and several strong-boxes. One of these was marked with a bank's identifying label. Once again he produced the series of skeleton keys. After a sharp tussle, as the lock turned halfway and was then disinclined to move farther, the steel case was open. He undid the leather bag inside, and gazed enthralled at the famous pearls. They shimmered and pulsated in the light, each one a perfect match: never had he seen anything so exquisite, so warm and beautiful. He sighed; then took the imitation pearls from his pocket and exchanged them for the genuine. He closed the door of the safe, shut the bookcase, relocked it — and chuckled. He had a clear fifty-five minutes in which to reach his car and return before it would be time to burgle the safe again.

"Good evening!"

Blackshirt spun round. By the door stood a man in a dressing-gown. In his hand he held a revolver.

It was so sudden and unexpected that for a moment Blackshirt could only stare. Was it possible that Janet had betrayed him he wondered. Then he discarded the thought. The jackdaw might do such a thing — but never Janet. Besides she would have too much to lose.

"Good evening," he replied mechanically.

"A strangely cultured voice for an uncultured profession! " The speaker moved forward a couple of paces. But at no time did the revolver waver.

The man took in Blackshirt's appearance more fully. "That's a strange garb you've got on. Black from head to toe... Good god! You're Blackshirt." His voice was excited.

"As good a name as any."

The man approached the table on which was a telephone. With his left hand he searched for the receiver. "You're the chap the papers are always writing up. The crook who's supposed to move in society. Be funny if you turned out to be Trotter-Smith." He had found the phone. Still his gaze never moved.

Blackshirt had one hope — to play for time. His hands were still by his side. Behind him lay the rifled safe, to his right a chair. Beyond those two articles, there was nothing within reach.

"I should need quite an amount of padding before I even resembled him," he replied. He moved his right foot tentatively.

"Keep still. I may not be a crack shot, but I'll hit you at this range. So you know Trotter-Smith! Maybe the papers are right." For the moment he had forgotten the phone. "Who the devil are you?"

"I also read the papers. The ex-Cabinet Minister is well known — for his paunch, if nothing else.' He transferred his weight to his right foot. Slowly, very slowly, he brought his left foot forward.

"I want to see your face; just in case I have had the misfortune to have seen you before, it will make interesting talk. Come on, take that hood off." The voice was harsh. He was some ten feet away. His left hand rested on the desk near the phone, he was half leaning against the desk, his feet on a carpet — the other end of which was now but three feet beyond Blackshirt.

"I'll wait. And as I don't know you, I very much doubt that you'll recognize me."

"Maybe I should have introduced myself!" the man said ironically. "My name is Darthweight — the owner of the house — and whatever you've taken from that safe… Damnation! The pearls. That's what you were after. Have you already…? Hand them back."

"You interrupted me before I had managed to get them."

Thanks to the other's annoyance Blackshirt had managed to transfer his weight again. His right foot was now only eighteen inches away. It was vital that Lord Darthweight didn't move. If he did…

"I'll damn well make certain. No, I won't. I suppose that's just what you'd like. For me to come close enough to you. What I'm going to do is to phone the police and let them find out. I'm staying right here." He lifted the receiver.

Blackshirt moved forward as if to intercede.

"Stay where you are! I don't want to shoot, but if you move again I shall not hesitate."

Blackshirt's foot was now touching the carpet. Less than eight feet separated the two men. "Did I set off an alarm that you turned up here so opportunely?"

Lord Darthweight paused. His left hand, holding the receiver, half-way to the dial of the phone. "I came down because I've got the toothache and I wanted a book to read. When I reached the door I saw the light; as I knew I had turned the lights out before I went to bed, there was only one answer. Rather humorous if you stop to think about it.

The notorious Blackshirt caught because someone had the toothache!"

"Very humorous." Now both feet were in position.

Lord Darthweight's index finger was inserted in the nine of the dial.

"Quick, Harry, grab him," shouted Blackshirt, raising his hands.

The revolver didn't move. "Clumsy," sneered the other, his gaze following the movement of Blackshirt's arms, "I expected something better from you."

"Such as this?" Blackshirt's right foot was under the edge of the carpet, his left on top. Gripping his heels together he threw himself backwards. The carpet slid along the floor and jerked the other's feet from under him. His head cracked against the edge of the desk and his unconscious body rolled on to the floor. The revolver skidded away.

Blackshirt stood up. The interruption had cost minutes of his precious time. Quickly he dragged the body through to the gun-room and over by one of the windows. Taking a handkerchief from the pocket of the dressing-gown he gagged Lord Darthweight, then bound his hands and feet with the belt. Satisfied the other would be unable to move without assistance, Blackshirt hid him behind one of the curtains. Back in the library he removed all traces of the struggle, then returned to the bathroom.

Having climbed down the drain-pipe he re-crossed the gravel patch, and returned to the car as quickly as he dared. There he slipped the bag containing the pearls into the side-pocket of the driving door, shut the car door, and returned the way he had just come.

He climbed into the bathroom for the second time, five minutes late, but as lar as he could judge there was no sign of Janet. Thirty minutes passed, and he began to think that something had gone wrong. He wondered if he had mistaken the rendezvous, and whether Janet had said they were to meet in the library. But no, he was certain she had said the bathroom. He waited yet another quarter of an hour, then decided to enter the library once more, in case he *had* been mistaken.

The door was shut. Because he could not remember having closed it when he left he gently eased back the catch and pressed. The door-hinges protested with a vague, muffled squeak, and Blackshirt grew rigid. Something warned him that all was not right. His sixth sense, developed during the years, was uneasy. Yet what could have happened? Deriding his fears, since there had been no further sound, he took a pace forward and fell flat on his face as his legs were caught up in a cord tied some two feet above the ground.

As he lay winded, two men seized him roughly by either arm and dragged him to his feet. A third flashed a torch in his face, and a well-known voice whispered with surprise, "Blackshirt! " For a moment Peebles was in a state of mental confusion.

Blackshirt's mind was also chaotic. What was Peebles doing here? Had Janet deliberately double-crossed him for the sheer delight of bringing the two together? And yet what could she hope to get out of it, since if the other suspected Janet, she certainly would gain nothing in respect of the pearls! And where was Janet? Not in the room so far as he could judge.

"What the hell are *you* doing here?" snarled Peebles. "So you did hear what we were intending to do, that night outside the door. By Christopher! Harry, you'll have something to answer for, after this! It's only because the three of us decided on tonight that we haven't lost the whole box of tricks to Mr. Interfering Blackshirt! "

'The three of us decided,' thought Blackshirt. Did that mean that they were putting a quick one across Janet, having obtained all the information they wanted from her? Was Peebles intending to double-cross Janet. The supreme humour of the situation made him laugh.

"What's so blasted funny?" demanded Jim, pressing the gun tightly into Blackshirt's side.

"What about Janet? Is she expecting you tonight?" asked Blackshirt.

"What if she isn't? I owe her one — for last time. And 1 owe you one, too. I told you to keep your nose out of my business, and I meant it. You came butting in here, so you can damn well pay for it! "

"Let me croak him," suggested Harry hopefully.

"Shut up, Harry. You've opened your trap too much already. Now Blackshirt, as you're here you can open this safe for us; then I'll fix it so you don't get in our way again. Take him up to the safe, boys, and make him do the work for us."

Unresisting, Blackshirt allowed himself to be led to the safe. While the outcome of the events might prove humorous, it certainly didn't look as though he, personally, would derive much laughter from them if Peebles carried out his unfinished threat — and the Jackdaw was not a man to do otherwise.

Blackshirt pretended to inspect the book-case which the other had indicated. Behind his hand he grinned. As he had left for the first time, so the others must have arrived — a regular shuttle service!

Then he bent down and re-cut the burglar alarm wires.

"Clever!" murmured the Jackdaw. "Damned if I won't feel almost sorry for you!"

Blackshirt worked in complete silence, his every move carefully watched. Taking much longer than he need, he racked his brain for a means of escape. What did the Jackdaw intend to do with him, once the pearls had been handed over? In all probability, lock him in the safe — it would appeal to the Jackdaw, since there was enough air to ensure his living until the following morning; and though he would not directly betray him to the police, which would go against the grain, it would be an ingenious way of getting rid of him.

If he tried to run for it the three men would, he knew, tackle him before he could move two paces — but, failing that, there was not a single thing he could do, bar shout for help.

The Jackdaw became impatient.

"Come on, you can open that old-fashioned junk quicker than this — no need to spend so much time on it."

Realizing that he could not hope to spin the job out any longer, Blackshirt opened the safe door. Peebles brushed him aside with a muttered warning to the others to watch him if they valued their skins. With a small steel tool the Jackdaw forced open the box; then, with a loud sigh of triumph, pulled out the bag of pearls and dropped them in his pocket.

As he did so an alarm bell raised its strident warning.

Chapter Six

The four men stared at each other. Jim and Harry cursed viciously, and showed signs of panic. The Jackdaw curtly ordered them to shut up and then, with an ironic gesture, raised his hands and smiled wryly at Blackshirt.

"Every man for himself!" he ordered.

Blackshirt felt a surge of admiration for the Jackdaw, who, like himself, was a fighter undismayed at the prospect of danger. Unscrupulous the other might be, often ruthless, yet ready to play the game — so long as it was played according to his own distorted rules, one of which was that no third party should interfere in the duel between Blackshirt and himself.

Meanwhile, what or who had set off the alarm bells? Janet? Blackshirt did not think so. More unscrupulous than Peebles she might be, and ready to iron out opposition to gain her own ends — yet she could have no ends to gain by rousing the household. No, it must have been someone else. It could be yet another housebreaker — but that would be stretching coincidence too far. Then Blackshirt remembered Lord Darthweight. Ten to one he had regained consciousness, and by some means had touched off the alarm.

Before Blackshirt reached the door, he heard the echo of distant voices, and sounds of movement.

"The damned household must all sleep as lightly as a feather." the Jackdaw grimly muttered. "Follow us, we've a ladder against the dining-room."

"For Pete's sake, come on!" Jim was not so phlegmatic.

Once in the passage Peebles and his companions ran towards the last room on the right-hand side, but as Blackshirt was about to follow he saw a body of men emerge from a side passage and make for him. Cut off from any chance of escape by the same route as the other three men, he hastily turned back into the library, slammed the door in the face of the leading pursuer, turned the key in the lock, and raced across to the door leading into the gun-room. This he also locked, and, with the speed of necessity, piled furniture against the two doors in a desperate endeavour to effect a temporary barricade.

If the noise were any indication the pursuing crowd, acting on the principle of a bird in hand, were concentrating on the library door, and ignoring the Jackdaw and his companions. This was cold comfort for Blackshirt, who ran to the window and looked out. A blaze of light from the lower rooms shone on the drive and revealed a number of men already gathering and pointing up at the room he was in. Invisible against a black background of curtain, Blackshirt searched for some means of escape. But, as he knew only too well, there was only one way of reaching the first floor of the main building: by ladder. The smooth walls offered no foothold — not that it would have been of help to him, since more and more people were collecting in the drive and on the lawn; and in the hands of at least one, Blackshirt saw a double-barrelled, ominous-looking sporting gun.

Then he looked upwards. There was a window directly above him, but unless he sprouted wings he realized he could not possibly bridge the intervening ten feet between himself and the sill. Not a single break in the mortar offered even the vestige of escape. Behind him he could hear an oak door splinter as an axe crashed through. Within seconds the men would burst in, and the identity of Blackshirt would at last be revealed as that of Richard Verrell, the popular novelist. There was but one thing he could do — step out on to the window-sill and spring upwards in the hope of reaching the top window-sill with his outstretched fingers. It meant a standing jump of at least four feet with nothing but smooth stone for a finger-hold — the attempt could mean almost certain death. Desperately he gauged his chances — and noticed something level with the top window-sill, which had previously escaped his observation. It appeared to be an iron bolt, projecting some six inches from the brickwork.

He drew back into the room, which resounded with the noise of blows. Slender as the chance might be, the bolt offered his only hope of escape. If he could lasso the bolt — if he had the rope to do it with! He chuckled as he compared his predicament with that of the tramp who wanted bacon so that he might have eggs and bacon if he had had some eggs...

The crowd on the lawn were amazed to see the lights in the library suddenly blaze out and reveal, outlined against the window, a figure in black frantically tearing at the curtains. They roared with excitement at the prospect of a man-hunt. They roared again when a car drove up and out rushed six policemen, who raced towards the house. With them was a man in plain clothes — the local detective-sergeant. He looked up, and, after momentary astonishment, recognized the black figure above.

"Blackshirt!" he cried with excitement.

The crowd heard him and for a second or two they were silent — then with increasing noise they roared and cheered. Blackshirt, the mystery cracksman whose exploits filled the front pages of newspapers time and time again; who was treated by some of the 'yellows' as a quasi-hero of the dashing 'Robin Hood' type. The excitement reached fever pitch. Blackshirt, the man who continually eluded every effort of the police to capture him; who seemed to be endowed with a 'will-o'-the-wisp' spirit; whom the police seemed powerless to capture! Blackshirt was almost in their hands; captured at Lodestone Manor! Small wonder they danced and shouted advice, and hindered the police who were trying to post themselves at various vantage spots.

Blackshirt stripped the curtains, and with a sigh of relief saw that the curtain-rods were of wood. He pulled one out of its socket, cut the sash cords, and tied the lengths together.

The door was giving way. The top panel was almost out, and he could see the faces of his pursuers gleaming with sweat as they thrust and pounded with axes, lengths of wood, anything they could lay their hands on, and fortunately, in their enthusiasm, hindering one another.

Working with frantic haste he cut a small notch in the top of the rod, tied a running bowline in the cord which he looped over the wood, then laid the two underneath the window-sill. Crossing the room again, he knelt down before an electric light plug attached to the skirting. Taking a pair of insulated pliers from his belt he thrust the ends into the two terminals in the plug. A bright flash and every light went out as the fuse parted.

The sudden darkness confused the men attacking the door. Silence followed the previous pandemonium, the men with axes feared to injure one another. He raced back to the window, leaned out backwards, and with his quickly made 'fishing rod' began to cast for the projecting bolt. Every second was precious. The crowd below were confused by the blackout, but he feared that one of them might at any moment produce a torch and flash it upwards. An action which would prejudice his already slim chance of escape, enabling the police to anticipate his next move.

Three times he cast upwards, but was unable to hook the bolt, and grimly he began to think he had misjudged the height of the bolt, and that it was beyond the reach of the curtain-rod. The attack on the door had recommenced and it could only be a matter of seconds before they broke through. It was when he had almost given up hope that he felt the knot engage and tighten. With a muttered prayer that the bolt would take his weight he gripped the rope with both hands, and swung out into space. Keeping his feet pressed against the wall he slowly pulled himself upwards.

Half-way up he heard the door below burst open; then shouts as the men eagerly raced into the room. As his outstretched hand grasped the window-sill he heard their cries turn to surprise, then rage, as they realized that their quarry had disappeared. To add to his troubles someone directed a torch at the house. A powerful beam lit up the library window, and then the black figure above. Exerting every last ounce of strength he gripped the sill with one hand, took the weight, and then released his hold on the rope. The sudden weight wrenched his shoulder and caused an agonizing pain, but ignoring it he raised his right hand level with the sill, and took another grip. With a quick heave he fell into the unlit room.

During the time that Blackshirt had taken to reach the window of the room above the library, the crowd on the lawn, including the police, had been silent, expecting that at any moment the figure would lose its grip and fall. It had seemed impossible that he could make it. But when the impossible had happened, Summers, in charge until his superior could be routed out of bed and arrive to take over, was galvanized into action. Arrest... and promotion seemed certain, but he had too often heard about the miraculous escapes of the daring cracksman not to study every possible precaution.

"Over here, quickly." The small group of uniformed police moved at the double towards the main door.

"Smith and Hoskins, stay outside and see if you can get some sense into this crowd. For heaven's sake stop them milling round like a bunch of sheep. Space them out right round. You've got torches, keep playing them over all the walls — tell anyone else whose got one to do the same." The two left, and soon their hoarse shouts could be heard.

"You others follow me." He raced inside and paused at the foot of the stairs.

"Jones, get the lights working. Grab hold of someone to tell you where the fuse box is... hey, you," he shouted at an elderly man, half dressed, with a bemused expression on his face.

"Yes, sir?"

"Who are you?" The man was too amazed to answer.

"Are you one of the staff?" said the other, cursing the fellow's stupidity.

59

"I, sir? I'm the butler, but I "

"Jones, take him! And you," he addressed the bewildered butler again, "when you've finished come up top. I'll want you handy."

"Phillips, Carter — how many staircases are there?" he bawled at the retreating butler.

"Two, sir. One here, one at the back."

"Phillips, Carter, one of you on each and follow us down, keeping on the staircase. Morgan, Bridges, follow me. We'll take the top floor and work downwards. Morgan, get hold of everybody in the house and bring them up top."

The sergeant raced up the stairs. In a very short time, Morgan joined him with four more men — those who had been hacking at the library doors.

The search began.

*

Blackshirt, on the third floor, looked out of a window and watched the crowd of men gradually form a cordon.

Beyond, the circle, Lord Darthweight was being revived in a manner that made the watcher chuckle. Two men supported him while a third chafed his limbs and was presumably being roundly sworn at for the pain he was causing. At the same time Darthweight was trying to swallow a cup of hot coffee, but thanks to his eager helpers was only able to appreciate half the liquid that was poured from the cup.

Reluctantly Blackshirt realized there was little chance of escape in that direction — or in any direction, if all the watchers were as alert. He weighed the chances of a quick dash. First, he would have to reach the ground floor, which would mean by-passing an unknown number of persons. Then he would have to rush forward, hoping that his sudden appearance would catch the line of men unawares long enough to enable him to pass through them. But even if he managed this, he saw, he would still have a long run before him, during which he might stumble over a root or some other obstruction.

The house was still dark, but at any moment the fuse would be mended. He might employ the same trick and cause yet another short, but if the detective knew his job — and it certainly seemed as if he did — there would be a man stationed by the fuse box ready for any repeat performance. Overhead he could hear the dull thud of regulation boots, interspersed with the 'slip-slap' of slippers, as the search continued. Voices kept calling out, checking that such and such a room had been searched.

Idea after idea flashed through his brain, each in turn discarded as unworkable. When the searchers reached the floor he was on, he would either have to move up or down. So far, he had only seen the one staircase, which was in front of the house. When the searchers had finished above, they would doubtless guard the staircase carefully, leaving him with but one choice — to move down. If they repeated the process, sooner or later he would be caught fast between the two jaws of the trap. 'Why,' he thought wryly, 'do they have to teach their men to be quite so systematic?' At that moment a beam from a torch waved across the front of the building, faintly illuminating the room he was in.

It was a small sitting-room, for the upper servants he imagined, with a settee, two arm-chairs, and some canvas folding seats, a couple of small tables and two telephones. With an old, well-used carpet this was all. But despite the bareness, he laughed — for an impossible scheme had occurred to him. One fraught with so many difficulties there was only a chance in a thousand of its succeeding. But worth trying…

*

At the top of the staircase on the fourth floor Summers called his searchers together. He was satisfied that their man had not come that far. About to give orders to proceed down, he paused as a man came running up towards him, whilst behind puffed the butler. It was the inspector, Marsh.

Rapidly Summers outlined the position to his superior. Then he turned to the butler.

"What about these confounded lights?"

"The constable is in the cellars now, sir. There was some difficulty in finding fuse wire. But as soon as I showed him the box he told me to come up here."

"You're certain this man is not on this floor?" asked Marsh.

"Yes, sir," replied Summers wearily, having answered the same question twice before.

"Sergeant, take the men down and keep on searching."

Half-way down the stairs a phone-bell rang.

"Where's the phone?" asked Marsh. "It's probably the Chief Inspector. I'll take it. Sergeant, come with me, in case he wants to know the position."

"In that room," answered the butler.

"Marsh speaking."

"Where the hell's that detective fellow? Get him at once, it's urgent."

"Here, Summers, find out what the crackpot wants."

"Summers here."

"What the devil are you still doing in the house? Do you mean to say you haven't got after him yet?" The sergeant's face went pale. He recognized the voice, it was Lord Darthweight, and enough had been said to prepare him for the worst. Marsh, watching, drew in his breath in a sharp hiss.

"What's wrong, sir?"

"Wrong! That infernal fellow's just walked out of the house dressed in an old suit of mine. Walked out and no one did a thing to stop him! Damn it all, you aren't still looking in the house are you? He's been chased into Farbut woods but " Summers slammed the receiver down.

"He's out, sir. In Farbut woods. Where are they?" he asked the butler in an explosive voice.

"Just at the end of the garden, sir. They aren't very big. About ten acres. In that direction." He pointed to the south.

"All right, Sergeant, I'll take over. Damn it, I thought you said you'd got the house ringed." Marsh's voice was harsh. "Call everyone together and tell 'em to search the woods. Blackshirt will probably make for the far side, so, Summers, you take the two cars and get round the back as fast as you can. I'll bring the rest through and round the side."

Thirty seconds later the two cars, with the butler guiding them, raced away along the drive. Bellowing instructions Marsh gathered those left together and leading them, raced southwards. Hardly a minute had passed since the phone call.

In the glare of the wavering torches a man was seen hobbling along between the house and the wood. Someone shouted out, his voice shrill from excitement, "That's the light grey suit Lord Darthweight was wearing yesterday. That's Blackshirt!"

In a mass they charged towards the figure and brought him down. Marsh tore up. "Got you," he cried eagerly, at the same time flashing his torch on the man's face. Then, "Lord Darthweight!"

"What in the name of all that's unholy…" His lordship's language was blistering. At last, when he had regained a measure of composure, "What is the meaning of this attack?"

"The men thought you were Blackshirt, my Lord."

"*Me*!" Darthweight spluttered. "Are you trying to tell me that I look like a confounded burglar — the Chief Constable shall hear about this."

"But after you telephoned to say that he had escaped in your clothes "

"*I* telephoned! I haven't been near a phone since that scoundrel knocked me out..."

But Marsh wasn't listening. Comprehending what had happened he raced back to the house...

*

Blackshirt hummed an *aria* from *Samson and Delilah*. His rendering was neither musical nor tuneful.

Happily he pressed the accelerator, and the powerful car increased speed. He had been lucky. For one thing he had spoken to Lord Darthweight and thus was able to give a near perfect imitation of his voice. Secondly, at the critical moment he had chanced upon a room possessing a telephone with a separate line for the use of the servants. And thirdly his guess had been correct. The detective had all along half-believed that he would escape. Therefore he had not been as prone to question the phone call as he might otherwise have been!

Soon the outskirts of London appeared. Row upon row of suburban villas, outlined for a moment by the car's powerful headlights. Street after street of uniform architecture. As five o'clock struck, Blackshirt parked the car not far from where he had originally found it. A quarter of a mile away was his own car — if no would-be burglar had used it on a night's escapade! All that now remained was for him to remove the pearls from the car pocket, adjust his hat at the usual rakish angle, ease the white scarf a little higher round his neck — and take his departure.

He opened the car pocket, and felt inside. To his amazement his hands met nothing save a piece of paper. Quickly he shone his torch inside the car to see if the leather pouch had fallen anywhere, then felt in the pocket to see if there were a hole. There was no hole — only a small square of paper which he withdrew. He smoothed the page down and read:

My dear Blackshirt,

You must admit my psychology is sound! Putting myself in your place I worked out just what I would do (rather involved here, but I hope you will understand what I mean) if I were going to help a lady who had once double-crossed me!

Remember, my dear, how clearly I itemized the habits of the household, stressing the hour of twelve as being the earliest that all would be clear. Staking my reputation that you would turn up early, I waited at the back of

63

the lawn opposite the little window you found so useful. From there I followed you to your car.

Chacun pour soi, if I remember my school days correctly.

Au revoir, Janet.

"Well I'm damned," murmured Blackshirt.

Chapter Seven

The next morning the popular papers headlined the news of the audacious burglary, and in vivid journalese informed their public of the latest outrage to law and order. The more staid papers referred deprecatingly to the whole incident, and dismissed it in a few short paragraphs; but the 'yellows', finding the news useful in a particularly dull period, did not hesitate to mix fiction with fact and produce 'copy' which held no punches.

The *Daily Star* was an example of the latter. Their ace reporter, Jameson, was not known for discretion.

INSOLENT BURGLARY
LORD DARTHWEIGHT'S PRICELESS PEARLS
STOLEN

During the night a series of fantastic happenings ruined the sleep of the entire staff of the famous old house, Lodestone Manor. Incredible as it may seem, a successful burglary resulted in the loss of the Darthweight pearls, so valuable that they could never be fully insured! And the name of the man responsible is known to the police I Yet they have arrested no one. The coup can be described as a brilliant success for Blackshirt.

Who has not heard of that name? Who has not read of his daring escapades, his brilliant successes time after time, in the field of crime? This paper has all too frequently had occasion to describe his astounding career, his iron nerve, and last but certainly not least, his apparent immunity from the police. We, as loyal citizens, pay rates and taxes every year to maintain a police force. Where does our money go? Certainly not towards capturing this elusive cracksman. The *Daily Star* would like to 'suggest' that somebody in office bestirred himself.

Our special reporter had an interview with a senior official of Scotland Yard and established the following facts. The unknown has been at large for many, many years — several famous collections of jewels have disappeared without trace, and it may be assumed that Blackshirt was responsible. Just one instance — the Roselea rubies.

He dresses in black, from head to foot. His skill is uncanny; whether entering a house or breaking open a safe. Those who have heard him speak say that he has a cultured, polished accent. Remarkable as it may seem, the man to whom our correspondent spoke had almost a note of admiration in his voice when he revealed that Blackshirt never carried a weapon but relied solely on his wits! This is a precis of the man who can successfully and continually defy our police.

The paper then went on to describe the burglary — but returned to the attack with a final paragraph.

Lord and Lady Carter are giving their annual ball next week — normally their guests would wear jewellery. Must they now appear without adornment for fear of theft by this audacious criminal? Or will the police for once provide adequate protection; thereby anticipating, instead of sweeping up afterwards?

Richard Verrell laughed joyfully. Mr. Jameson must possess imagination allied with a strong sense of public duty, he decided. And if the overworked police didn't receive a rap over the knuckles, especially since the papers had begun a 'no-good-police-force' campaign, he would give up crime!

Curiously enough, in the newspaper reports very little mention was made of the fact that others had been unlawfully present the previous night, and that they had successfully escaped before the 'real fun' had begun. And only one paper reported that a nursemaid was missing from the household. Blackshirt was the star attraction!

With a wry smile Verrell read one part of the report which was incorrect. The paper endowed him with the Roselea rubies and the Darthweight pearls — neither of which in fact, he possessed — though indeed, he had worked extremely hard for both!

He had now twice been over-trumped, each time by a woman, each time by the same woman — Janet! He remembered how carefully he had planned, the troubles he had overcome, to remove the fake pearls from the show-room. He had then planted them, fairly certain that once he had openly removed them from the safe Janet, as unscrupulous as it was possible to be, would make a play for them. How successfully, he now realized! For the second time his innate sense of humour battled with his anger — and humour won the day.

At that moment Roberts entered the room. "A Colonel Peebles would like to see you, sir."

Verrell chuckled. "Show him in, Roberts."

Peebles ignored his host's outstretched hand. His face was angry. "I want to see you alone," he said with emphasis.

"I see you've been reading your press cuttings," he snorted as soon as Roberts had left the room.

"They've done me rather well," replied Verrell pleasantly. "Though they're not always accurate."

"Damn the truth. Do you know how much it cost me to arrange everything?"

"Can't say I do."

Peebles clenched his fists. "It cost me a sight more than I can afford. Harry and Jim want their money regularly, come sun or hail. That wretched housekeeper wouldn't come across under twenty-five quid. Janet wanted fifty because she said she had to have a suitable wardrobe. Then there was what I had to pay out to get the information in the first place — if it cost less than three hundred I'll become a village parson. I spend all that, and then what happens? Mr. ruddy Blackshirt pokes his nose in, and in spite of my warning. All that trouble for you to reap the benefit."

"To tell the truth I thought you were turning up the following night. If you had done as you'd arranged, then I shouldn't have bothered you, should I?" he asked in a patient tone.

Peebles choked with rage. His instinct was to throw himself at his host, but there was something about the expectant attitude of Verrell that warned him not to try.

"Besides.' continued Verrell as he relaxed, "you have the pearls so why worry?"

"Yes, I have the pearls. I took them home and had a look at them. After nearly being cornered by a bunch of yelling rustics, having to change cars because that fool Jim grabs one with a petrol tank half empty — after all that, what do you think I found?"

"Perhaps," suggested Verrell mildly, "they were false."

"The damned things weren't worth more than a couple of bob. The famous Darthweight pearls a fake!" He had been intent on his own grievance, but suddenly his voice grew sharp. "How did you know? You only saw them from a distance?" He thrust his right hand in his coat pocket.

"I put the false pearls in the safe approximately an hour before you took them out." He smiled.

It was more than Peebles could bear. With an oath he pulled out a small automatic and levelled it. "I'll give you one minute to hand them over.

Otherwise I'll blast your brains out." His rage had carried him beyond the point of discretion.

"I haven't got them." Verrell spoke coolly.

Despite himself, Peebles was convinced. Slowly he lowered the gun. "If you haven't got them, who has? The papers said nothing about their having been recovered."

"I'm here. You're here. There's one person missing."

"What the — do you mean that — Janet's got them?" His voice rose again.

"So she told me in a note she left. But perhaps I'd better explain!" Shortly Verrell described what had happened the previous night.

Peebles relaxed into a chair. He rubbed his hand across his forehead. "So that's why she hasn't turned up to claim her share. And I thought she was playing square for once."

"Or that you'd fixed it so that she had to play fair?"

"What the hell you can find in it to laugh at beats me! If I ever get my hands on her I'll break her neck. That's twice. I ought to have known better than to trust that miserable little double-crosser."

"And yet," said Verrell, a twinkle in his eye, "I believe you intended to do just that."

Peebles grunted savagely.

"Stay and have some coffee. Roberts was about to bring some in, I'll tell him to make some more."

Peebles did not reply, but stayed frowning at the carpet, his face set in an ugly expression. Verrell took this as an affirmative reply.

When prevailed upon, Peebles had breakfast and when he had finished and was smoking a cigarette he half smiled.

"Maybe Janet's got the pearls now, but she won't get very far this time."

"How's that!" queried Verrell with interest.

"The day before she left for the country I got one of the boys to grab her passport."

"What perfect trust on all sides!"

"So she'll have to stay in this country until they'll issue another one — and that takes several days, if not longer." His voice had lost its harshness. "Verrell, I think we've got her." He ended excitedly. He leaned forward. "For once I think it's time we worked together. Forget the past and concentrate on finding Janet. She can't get abroad to sell those jewels because she's got no passport "

"Easily find a spiv to sell her one."

"They want anything over a hundred quid today. Things are getting tight for people who want to leave unnoticed. And that's the point I'm getting at. Whether she waits until the passport office issues a new one, or tries to buy one, she needs money, and quite a bit of it. There's only one way she can sell the pearls and that's through a fence. If you and I visit all the big fences we know — a small one wouldn't handle such stuff — maybe we can get a lead on her. And then — — " He squeezed his hands together.

Verrell knew precisely who Peebles imagined would be the senior party in any such arrangement. He would be expected to pass on any information received, whilst Peebles would pass on precisely nothing.

"What will you do if you find out where she's staying?"

"What do you think I'd do? I'll get those pearls back if it's the last thing I ever do."

"She may quite possibly have sold them by that time."

"No. She'll get twice the price on the Continent. What she'll do is to sell one or two — just enough to have some ready cash."

"Why don't you let her keep them — after all, she won them fairly!"

"Blackshirt, you're the most — quixotic fool I've ever met. You seem bewitched by her! I'm not going to rest until I've got them. Are you coming in with me, or not?"

Verrell thought for a few seconds. There was nothing to be lost by such an arrangement; and there might be much to gain.

"Fair enough! I'll talk with one or two people I know and see if they can give me any sort of lead. What arrangements shall we make for getting in touch with each other?" "I'll drop round in a couple of days' time. Well, I'm off. Thanks for the breakfast. But remember, Blackshirt, maybe I don't dislike you personally, but if you cross me again, heaven help you!" He clapped his hat on to his head and with a muttered good-bye strode out of the flat.

Thoughtfully Verrell smoked a cigarette before starting his morning's work. Offhand he knew of only one fence big enough to handle the pearls; he decided to visit him as soon as possible. Apart from any other consideration he was not averse to seeing Janet again!

The evening papers were full of the burglary, though few new items of interest had come to hand. The police, stung by the morning editions, had stated that it was more than possible an early arrest would occur, though they declined to say on what grounds. It was a face-saver. Marsh and

Summers had found to their cost just how little evidence they could offer the irate Assistant-Commissioner.

But there was one paragraph that did interest Blackshirt. There was a description of a ball shortly to be given by Lord and Lady Carter in honour of their daughter's coming-out and special mention was made of the protection to be given by the police against any recurrence of the daring burglary of the night before. A special force of constables would be provided to patrol the grounds and building, although on her own initiative Lady Carter was employing several private detectives. The writer went on to say that he doubted if any house had ever been so well guarded, and categorically stated that the newspaper would give a whole issue over to comic strips should the intrepid Blackshirt succeed in breaking in. Even should he achieve the impossible, then he would be trapped — as a result of various precautions which could not be revealed.

'*No*,' the article ended, '*Blackshirt will not be a guest at the ball*.'

Richard Verrell forgot Janet as he read this article. A challenge was of all things the most likely to rouse him, and kindle that spark of adventure and lust for danger which two centuries before would have made him a successful buccaneer.

*

The two-seater Healey sped through the countryside. Growing corn, still green in its immaturity, provided a wonderful splash of colour. Fruit had formed on the trees, but was not yet large enough to pick. Animals moved in leisurely fashion round the fields, searching for extra succulent tit-bits.

Parkgate House was in the heart of the country. Some two miles from the nearest village, it was Georgian, with large state rooms, a perfect setting for any social event. The house had belonged to the same family for several generations, and had been maintained in excellent condition.

These facts Verrell already knew from the papers, but he was more immediately concerned with the general outline of the house, the lay of the surrounding countryside, and, if possible, the precautions that were being taken against unlawful entry — and exit.

At the village of Plucklode he parked his car outside the local inn and, as the hour was one during which the laws of England generously permitted him to enter and drink on the premises, he went in and ordered a pint of ale. In his normal, easy manner he was soon deep in conversation with the bartender, and gradually brought the conversation round to the subject that must have been engrossing the whole neighbourhood, so eager was the other man to speak.

From the twenty minutes of conversation Verrell was able to glean little of real importance. The previous day workmen had started to build a temporary wire fence right round the house. This enclosed the lawns and ornamental gardens. On either side of the fence was a clear space which could be easily and efficiently patrolled. According to some workmen who had stepped in for a quick one, the fence consisted of a number of wires so placed that no one could crawl through them, so high that they could not be cleared by jumping, and it was to be electrified and illuminated by flood-lighting. There would be only one pair of gates, controlling the main drive.

More than that the man did not know. Verrell led the conversation back to crops for the last five minutes, then left, remarking that he might spend an hour or so looking round before he continued on his way up north.

He walked briskly along the winding road to Parkgate House. The air was fresh, and the exercise made his blood tingle with well-being. Presently he turned to the right, and entered the main drive leading to the house. Three hundred yards farther on he was hailed by a man who eyed him suspiciously.

"What d'you want?"

"Just what has that to do with you?"

At the sound of Verrell's voice, the other touched his cap and apologized. "Sorry, sir, but I've orders to inquire as to what anyone is doing round these parts."

"Why?"

"Well, sir, as this here road only leads to Parkgate House, in a manner of speaking it might be called private, and no one's allowed here what ain't a right."

"I came along this way to have a look at the house. The man at the pub informed me this was the way."

"I'm sorry, sir, but no one is allowed nearer the house than this who ain't got a pass."

Verrell laughed. "It all sounds very melodramatic. Are the people in the house conducting secret atomic experiments or something?"

"Thank you, sir." The man accepted a cigarette. "In a manner of speaking, yes, sir. Except that it's nothing to do with atoms. It's all on account of that there Blackshirt fellow. I don't know if you've heard of him?"

71

"Vaguely."

"He's that cracksman all the papers has been talking about, sir."

"Oh yes, of course! He's just committed a burglary somewhere or other!"

"That's right. Lady Carter is givin' a ball next week and all these precautions are to make sure he don't pinch anything that night. If you wouldn't mind telling me what you want, maybe I could manage it. Though if you don't know his Lordship, you won't be allowed in."

"It was only a very small item. I intend writing my new novel about this district. I wanted to have a look round here as I thought I might bring the house into it."

"Do you write, sir?"

"Yes, Verrell's the name."

"Not *the* Richard Verrell, sir?"

"My name is Richard Verrell."

The man's distrust and suspicion immediately disappeared as he eagerly discussed Verrell's books. Agog at meeting one of his favourite authors — his first favourite, he stoutly declared — he offered personally to escort Verrell up to the fence and pass him through. "He might let you look around, sir, though natural-like I couldn't say for certain that he would."

"Good lord! I wouldn't dream of troubling him. I only need the general lie of the land. Anyway, what's all this about — er — Blackshirt? Do you really think he will turn up next week?"

The guard led Verrell up the drive and took him round the perimeter of the wire fence, which was nearly completed.

At first he was cautious in what he said, only detailing the obvious. But under Verrell's charm he thawed and described at full length the precautions being taken.

The electrified barrier was to be patrolled, with guards inside and out. Detectives would be present in the house itself under the guise of waiters. Every room not being used during the evening was to be locked and connected to a modern burglar alarm guaranteed to make a noise audible at many hundreds of yards. The guests were to be admitted by special invitations only and to make sure there would be no chance of forgery the Carters had had them engraved on watermarked cards. Furthermore, almost every guest would be personally known to his hosts. Even if Blackshirt should, by some fluke, enter the grounds, once the alarm was given there was not a chance of his escaping. The plans for such an emergency were fool proof.

Verrell, having learned as much as he could without awakening suspicion, changed the subject by asking the man to point out some of the well-known places round about. Finally he promised to send an autographed copy of the book that was to feature Parkgate House. The guard was profuse in his thanks.

As he drove back to London his mind was occupied by what he had just learned. Unless the man had been romancing, and there seemed no reason to suppose he was, it appeared completely impossible to break into Parkgate House — and even more impossible, once in, to break out! As far as he could see, there was not a single loophole in the defences. Once, confronted by similar circumstances, he had entered the grounds suspended between the axles of a car, but even if he tried that ruse once more and effected an entry — there was no way of escape. Not merely patrols inside the barrier, but outside as well, and the man had even mumbled a word about watch-dogs — before he closed his mouth he had taken a quick look at Verrell.

By the time he reached his flat, he was depressed. It seemed that for once a reporter had stated the truth. Blackshirt would not be present — if he valued his liberty. Feeling in need of company to cheer him up, he decided to dine out at his club, the Junior Aits. After an hour's work, he walked the short distance between his flat and the dub.

In the bar, Verrell met several men he knew, and after a few cocktails they decided to go in to dinner together. As they made their way towards the door two men entered, one of whom hailed Verrell.

"Hallo there I Haven't seen you in a month of Sundays. Are you just going in to dinner?" Oakley was the leader writer for one of the big daily papers. "What have you been doing with yourself?"

"Just back from the south of France. Had three or four weeks over there. Funnily enough I met Stephen."

"Give me an author's job any day," muttered Oakley mournfully. "Every time I meet you, you've just come back from somewhere or other. I haven't had a holiday in years," he complained. "But I'm forgetting. Verrell, this is Lancy, George Lancy. Had the bad taste the other day to say he enjoyed your books."

The two men shook hands.

"Look, what are you going to have?"

"I've just had two," protested Verrell, "we're on our way in to dinner."

"Never mind that! There's time for a quick one, and I'll tell Jules to fix up another two places."

Later the three joined the others at the table. Oakley was well known, and as soon as someone mentioned that Lancy worked for the same paper, Verrell placed him. He was a younger son of one of the big families, and, though in receipt of a private income, wrote to supplement it. Every morning the paper printed an article of some thousand words with out-of-the-way bits of information, very short biographies of people who were in the news that day, or description of any big event. Lancy, assisted by one other writer, was responsible for this. His position made him very suitable, since he was on fairly intimate terms with many of the 'big names' and was invited to most of the socially important dances and receptions. Despite the fact that he wrote personalities, he did not descend to ferreting out and printing details that would have been an embarrassment to the person concerned — in other words he left scandal severely alone.

But if he withheld such interesting information from the public, he relaxed in his present company and soon had the table roaring with laughter.

"Covering the Carter do?" asked a man along the table.

"As a matter of fact I am. The editor knows someone who knows someone and he managed to get me an invite. Personally, I couldn't care less. I'll hardly know a soul there, and in any case they're much too hounds and horse for my liking. Half of them turn up in red coats and prance round as if still at a hunt! The only reason I'm going is in case this Blackshirt fellow makes a try. Lot of stuff and nonsense in my opinion."

"Hardly that," disagreed Oakley mildly. "I wouldn't call electric fencing, watermarked invitation cards and so on a mare's nest. You mark my words, George, you'll have some fun there yet."

"Do you honestly think this cracksman will be fool enough to turn up knowing all the precautions that are being taken? Probably be fast asleep in bed instead of inviting the police to march him off."

Another man joined in. "That's the whole point. This fellow seems to walk in and out of where he likes, so the police put their heads together and decided to use a little psychology. They've made the place absolutely impregnable. I was talking to a chap only today who's had a hand in it, and he said nothing could get in or out of the place unseen. But the police asked the papers to publish some of the facts, as a kind of dare. One of the higher-ups decided that if they said Blackshirt could not get in — then

Blackshirt would have a bash. Seems damn' silly to me! Who the deuce would charge along there knowing full well what was in store?"

"If I were Blackshirt," said Verrell, "I would keep as far away as possible."

The conversation soon changed to politics, when it became heated.

Verrell returned home, took off his jacket, donned an old and comfortable dressing-gown, lit a cigarette and relaxed in an arm-chair. An idea was running through his mind… so daring that it *might* succeed!

The pile of ash in the ash-tray increased as the night grew shorter.

*

Parkgate House was a blaze of colour. Lanterns were festooned round the grounds, every light in the house was on, and, in addition, the electrified fence was lit completely round its perimeter by powerful flood-lights. Not one patch of land inside the fence was in darkness.

Guards patrolled the fence at frequent intervals, some with large watch dogs attached to leads. At the gate men checked the cars and their occupants as they drove up," one inspected the invitation closely, by holding it up to a light to check the watermark before returning it to the owner with a request that it be retained and produced on departure. Those who grumbled at such precautions were politely but firmly informed that it was entirely for their own benefit.

When that check was over, another man came forward, and stood on the running-board while the car was driven to the main entrance, where each guest was announced. In addition, the butler had orders to make certain that the number of people arriving by car was the same as that enumerated on the invitation — there was to be no risk of Blackshirt's smuggling his way through the gate, and then openly entering the house. Cars were parked to the right of the house and, if chauffeur-driven, the man was escorted back through the gates and shown the lodge where he might obtain a meal and a drink — the cracksman was to have no chance of remaining within the wire fence if he were masquerading as a chauffeur. If the owner of the car was driving, he parked it before being escorted to the door, and was watched until he had passed the butler.

To the younger members of the company it was all in the nature of a tremendous lark. Many were the heavily humorous comments addressed to the guards who stood by the gates to the door; comments accepted with a philosophic grin.

Inside, the atmosphere was one of gaiety, where Ruritanian precautions were forgotten. One or two of the servants were somewhat clumsy, and not very adept when it came to serving champagne — but those who noticed politely ignored such failings.

Lord and Lady Carter were worried. When such stringent precautions had first been suggested they had demurred. But even when they had at last agreed, they were unprepared for such a highly organized system and it left them startled and bewildered. Nevertheless, since their guests took it all in good humour they relaxed, and the party went with a swing.

In the meantime Blackshirt was enjoying himself.

Chapter Eight

He had driven up to the grounds in a car which had not yet been missed by its real owner. The guards at the gate passed him through, after carefully ascertaining that the card, inviting Mr. George Lancy, was genuine. He had relied on that — but the first moment of suspense was when his name was announced by the butler. Lancy had said very few present would know him, but it needed only one of those few to be near the door to discover that Lancy wras not Lancy, and then… But his luck held. Lord Carter's welcome was polite but disinterested — his wife's also.

Three large rooms were being used, running the length of the house. The centre one was the ballroom, where a well-known dance band were seated on a raised dais. To the right was the bar, where wrhite-coated waiters were ready to serve any kind of drink that might be requested. On the left was a smaller room, where a continuous buffet was served.

Blackshirt had several dances before moving to the refreshment room. Here he partook of a light snack, not without a mental query as to whether this would be his last meal in public for some time to come.

There was still a feeling of excitement among the guests. They watched the clock, and wondered if the cracksman would be daring enough even to try to gain admittance — or whether he had chosen the wiser course and stayed away. At frequent intervals women glanced down to make certain that their jewellery was still intact; the men in turn watched those whom they were escorting to see that nothing untoward happened.

As the evening wore on and nothing occurred, the tension eased and the general verdict was that, after all, the night would be quiet. The guests relaxed, and only the 'heavy-handed' waiters remained alert. As Blackshirt moved round the floor with a charming young girl, he decided that Lancy had been wrong in saying the party would be boring. Admittedly, some of the women looked a little 'tough', as though five-barred gates were only incidental obstacles; and some of the men did blow their hunting-horns in the more boisterous numbers; but at least they were all enjoying themselves whole-heartedly — not in the bored fashion of nightclub London.

"A penny for them. That is, if they're not worth more!" Betty, his partner, interrupted his thoughts.

"I'm sorry, I was miles away. Just thinking how well everybody is enjoying the evening.

"Yes — but I wish this burglar would get a move on and turn up."

Blackshirt grinned. "That's rather a peculiar wish, isn't it? You wouldn't want to see your friends robbed?"

"Of course not — but think how thrilling it would be to see this man. I've read all the papers and, maybe I'm an incurable romantic, but I've got the feeling that he must be rather a nice man. Like you, for instance!"

"Thank you, kind lady," he replied laughingly.

"Oh! I didn't mean to compare you, but it's just that I was trying to express my thoughts. The papers hinted that he robbed for the fun of it — I wonder if they're right." "You would probably find him unshaven, dirty and disreputable. And most vicious. I don't doubt he beats his wife three times a week!"

"Now you're making fun of me." She pouted. "And I bet he's tall, dark and handsome."

Verrell hastily changed the conversation. "Who is that lady over there? I seem to recognize her."

As soon as the number was over he saw his partner to her seat, and left. Much as he would have liked to dance with her again it was no part of his plan that anyone should remember him. He was banking on the fact that, if nothing was responsible for fixing his features in anyone's mind, when inquiries were made no one present would remember him — or, if they did, would be unable to describe him.

There were some wonderful pieces of jewellery being worn that evening. He longed to be able to handle them, to have the sensuous pleasure of gazing into the depths of the pearls with their soft, warm tints; or the hard, glittering brilliance of the diamonds. Lady Carter and her husband had at one time lived in India. A maharajah had given her a necklace, with several large stones and hundreds of smaller ones, that must have been worth a fabulous amount. The ring on her finger was magnificent. Yet so elegantly was she dressed that her jewels were in no way ostentatious. Other women were wearing similar, if somewhat less opulent ornaments. It was not the money these jewels represented that interested Blackshirt. If a silver cup were of exquisite chasing and proportions he would prefer it to a similar article in gold, which was otherwise clumsy and ugly.

He looked at his watch, which he had checked with the wireless before he had left home. Half past two. In half an hour's time he would be working to a schedule of seconds. Slowly the minutes ticked by, and he felt that surge of excitement which was to him what opium is to the drug addict. At two-fifty-five, he moved out of the corner of the room where he had been enjoying a cigarette. Hidden in his right hand was a minute pair of wire-cutters which, despite their size, would cut through any clasp with ease.

The dance was a slow fox-trot. The lights had been turned low — but not too low. The detectives in the room had, by now, come to the same conclusion as the guests.

Blackshirt had not and would not turn up. No man would enter the grounds, knowing as he must do the painstaking precautions and many traps. So at regular intervals, one at a time, they disappeared. When they came back they wiped their mouths contentedly.

"No, Bert, he ain't coming. Still, even if he don't, at least he's given us a cushy night's work. Just standing 'ere, and watching them swells dance around. What couldn't you and me do with some of the sparklers they're wearing?" asked one of the private detectives.

Bert was by way of being a socialist. "It ain't right they should be allowed to have them. What have they done to earn them?"

"Darn! If they hadn't got them, you wouldn't be here tonight earning a few quid with plenty to eat and drink, and nothing to do!"

Just then: "My necklace — it's gone. I've been robbed," screamed an elderly lady.

"My pearls. John, my pearls! " echoed another.

The band stopped abruptly.

The dancers remained frozen, grotesquely holding their position.

Blackshirt had struck.

*

The guards moved with speed. An alarm bell was sounded, and the gates were locked. An inspector raced into the ballroom and rapidly gave orders.

"I must ask no one to move. Blackshirt has somehow made his way here tonight, and committed at least two robberies. If we may have your co-operation we will soon capture him."

The guests stayed where they were, looking about them and wondering which guest would turn out to be the elusive criminal. All the doors were guarded. Some of the guests had moved outside to enjoy a snatch of fresh air, and they were respectfully asked to return indoors.

Blackshirt looked at his watch. Five minutes to go. Had he timed it correctly? It depended on how fast the police moved.

"At the moment," the inspector said, "a search is being made of the grounds, and the rest of the house. Should no trace of the burglar be found I am afraid that I'll have no choice but, with Lord Carter's permission, to institute a search." It was quite plain that he did not think Blackshirt would be found anywhere but among the guests present.

Two minutes still remained. A man rushed up to the inspector. "There's no one outside, sir, and no one has passed through the gate."

Then another uniformed man reported. "No one in the house, sir."

The inspector's face became grim. "Lord Carter," he said, "I am afraid it will be necessary to search the guests."

"But — but you can't do that! I mean to say "

"I am very sorry, my lord, but Blackshirt is somewhere in this room." There was a gasp as people for the first time fully realized the implication. "And since I am certain you would wish to aid the police, a search will be necessary. If the men will move to the right, and the ladies to the left, we will get this unfortunate business over as soon as possible."

Rather sheepishly the people divided.

At that moment the noise of a distant aeroplane engine was heard. And from somewhere, nobody at first could say quite where, an eerie sound rose and fell. With their nerves already strained by events, people shifted uncomfortably — it almost seemed as if a disembodied spirit were wailing! The elderly lady, who had first given the alarm, moaned. The inspector racked his brains in an effort to puzzle out what this interruption meant. Was it part and parcel of some plot of Blackshirt's — or was it coincidence — or was...?

"Sir, the plane — someone's shouting from it." A man ran in from the garden.

In three strides the inspector passed outside. With one accord, the guests flocked after him, despite cries from the guards asking, and in some cases ordering, them to stay where they were. The front lawn became a mass of people in evening dress. The guards redoubled their vigilance as they patrolled the fence. Dogs eagerly sniffed the air as they padded behind their masters.

Overhead a small helicopter slowly descended. Both sides were a mass of illuminated bulbs, spelling out the word BEZE. The voice that had so startled everyone resolved itself into a man speaking through a loud-hailer.

"Eat Beze Honey. It is guaranteed to be the most nutritious honey on the market. Have some at breakfast, lunch, tea and some before you go to bed. Eat Beze…" The voice grew louder and louder as the plane descended.

It seemed as if the plane were actually going to land. The inspector waved his fist, and yelled at the pilot to move away. One of his subordinates conscientiously took the number.

"I'll get him for this," swore the inspector, "bringing his blinkin' advertising stunt over this house. It's the last time he ever takes the air! Tell him to clear away — tell him to go."

But his men were as helpless as he was to make themselves heard above the deep boom of "Eat Beze Honey."

The crowd was milling around, some shouting, some laughing.

"Eat Beze Honey," roared the loud-speaker.

And then a rope-ladder was lowered over the side. The inspector was the first to realize what was happening. "Keep back, keep back!" he shouted at the top of his voice. Blackshirt's going to try and get away by plane. Hey! There he goes! Catch him!"

Blackshirt raced for the ladder, now only three feet above the ground. A white scarf was wound round his face hiding the lower half, and a cap pulled down well over his head left only his eyes visible. Over his clothes he wore a black, light-weight raincoat.

He had a fifty-yard lead, and was congratulating himself as he made for the ladder, when suddenly it rose beyond his reach. The pilot had misjudged his level! Two men, running at full speed, were but thirty yards behind. The plane was fifty yards nearer the gate before the pilot corrected his mistake and again lowered the helicopter towards the ground.

From the fence came the sharp bark of a dog. It came leaping forward, its jaws open, fangs showing. Fifty, forty, thirty, twenty yards until the dog was almost on him… and there was still another fifteen yards to go. With the speed of desperation he tore his raincoat off and wrapped it round his right fist. The manoeuvre lost him ground. A plainclothes detective was almost on him, hand outstretched. The inspector bellowed, "Jump to it, cover the plane. One of you take charge of it." But his voice could not compete against the roar from overhead, "Lunch, tea, and before you go to bed…"

Blackshirt could hear the panting behind him, and a hand clutching for his shoulder. At that moment the dog sprang. With his right fist he thrust the coat into the dog's mouth — the beast gave a choking sound and fell on its back. In a minute it had worried the cloth out of its mouth with its paws and was on its feet, ready to attack again.

Then, twisting like an eel, Blackshirt turned, his left hand whipped forward. The man fell backwards, and landed heavily on the ground.

Breathlessly, Blackshirt clutched a rung of the rope-ladder. As the plane rose a second man leaped upwards, and caught the lowest rung with both hands.

As quickly as he could Blackshirt climbed into the plane. He gave rapid instructions to the pilot. The other grinned, and nodded his head. The detective, holding on grimly with both hands, tried to raise himself rung by rung — but found the plane's motion and his own weight too much!

The crowd, after the first wild shouts of surprise, indignation, and in some cases sheer joy of the unusual, turned silent as they saw the man vainly wriggling at the end of the ladder. All of them realized that it would take little to cause a tragedy.

The inspector had sent subordinates running off to phone the Yard, and check on the plane's identity — any action to postpone for a minute the awful fact that he had failed. Now he grimly watched the hovering plane. What would Blackshirt do? Would he continue, regardless of the man's life — would he add murder to his other crimes?

The plane was descending. Men rushed towards it, but only to stop short — at the ornamental lake.! Two cuts severed the ropes. A mighty 'splash' as water sprayed out in all directions, soaking everyone round about. The detective scrambled to his feet in four feet of rather smelly water. A newt slithered down the back of his neck.

*

The director of the 'Okay' advertising company groaned. The pilot of the helicopter ordered by the director groaned. Both said they wished they had never undertaken the job.

Irate police officials made certain pertinent remarks.

The pilot, "I keep telling you, five miles from the house he asked to be put down — he'd paid, so why not? How was I to know you wanted to see him?"

The director, "Listen, gentlemen, I do a lot of good business. I own one of the best, most upright — O.K., O.K. — that's the firm's name, ha! — if you don't want to hear my story — I get a phone call; will I arrange to send a plane, advertising Beze Honey, over the house at such and such a time? How much will it cost? The money is sent round in one pound notes

82

— and I do *not* know who brought them. I am to give orders, so. A man is to be picked up, who will have been handing round leaflets. It is essential to get the name Beze well known. Why *should* I be suspicious? In the advertising world..."

*

It was obvious that, in their previous description of Blackshirt's prowess and impudence, the papers had been under a restraining influence. For now they searched through the Thesaurus for every possible simile — and used them! The *Daily Star*, in particular, thundered against the police, and applauded Blackshirt for being so cunning as to avoid their hasty and ill-conceived snares. Jameson, again responsible for the article, was ordered to visit George Lancy and obtain all the copy he could — then go forth and capture Blackshirt... without the aid of the bungling police. Jameson did as he was told, but was not quite so confident of his ultimate success as his superiors might have wished.

Every paper had cleverly reconstructed the manner in which the crime had been committed, immediately it was known that Lancy, instead of attending the ball as had been supposed, was in actual fact, stretched out on his bed recovering from the unpleasant effects of chloroform. Lancy's flat was besieged, first by the police then by a mob of eager reporters. These invasions did nothing to soothe his ruffled feelings. Thus, when Jameson rang the doorbell, Lancy was anything but civil. He tried to slam the door, but the other hastily inserted a foot.

"As one newspaper man to another"

Lancy indicated that all newspaper men could go to the same place. Besides, he had never liked the little he knew of Jameson.

"Have a heart. The old man sent me out to see you and if I don't get copy I shall get the sack."

"For Pete's sake come off that rubbish," said Lancy wearily. "If you don't get it, you make it up. Buzz, and go use your imagination."

"You know the *Daily Star* is offering a reward of one thousand pounds to anyone who gives information leading to the capture of this Blackshirt?"

"So what? And would you please move your foot."

"So a half share of that is five hundred."

"And?"

"I think you know enough to come in on half. Look here, be reasonable, and come across the way. A couple of stiff ones is what you need; clear away that head."

Lancy hesitated, which was sufficient for the reporter to push the door farther open, couple his arm with the other's, and lead the way across the street.

The Bottle had no pretensions. It was a small pub, no more. Its inside was as murky as the past of some of its customers, but along one wall were a series of booths where a man could talk in safety. That was why Jameson chose it.

One double gin was quickly followed by another, and together they did something to soothe Lancy's ruffled feelings.

"Tell me, Lancy, have you got any ideas as to who this Blackshirt fellow is? What he looks like?"

"I've told fifty coppers and a hundred reporters already that I haven't got the faintest."

"What exactly happened?"

"I was dressing, adjusting my tie when in the mirror I saw a black shadow. I turned, but before I was half-way round a pad of that damned stuff was shoved over my nose. I struggled, but he's got muscles like steel and the next thing I knew was being ill — tied down on my bed. Beyond that I can tell you nothing. So if you'll excuse me "

"Hang on," said Jameson in silky tones. He called for another round of drinks. "The paper's offering this reward. The editor told me to go out and capture Blackshirt — if I do I take the cash."

"Just like that!"

"If you could set me off on the right track, then half would be yours."

"And what makes you think that you'll be successful when the police have failed for years?" His voice was scornful.

Jameson was unruffled. "What I want you to do is to go over the past few weeks with me. At some time or other you've been in Blackshirt's company."

"Damn it! Do you think I run around with crooks all day long. Because if you do " He had half risen in his rage.

"I don't think you do anything of the sort — knowingly. Let's add up the score, then you'll see why. Blackshirt moves in society. We know that — he's as good as admitted it at times. Anyone who's heard him speak has said he's got an educated voice. He's got brains, is clever. That means that when he moves round normally, he's probably a most charming person — the last person one would connect up with a cracksman. He might be anyone."

"That's helpful!"

"But it is someone who knew you were going to the Carters' ball — that narrows things a bit. Who have you met lately who knew you were going?"

"A few dozen people. I mentioned it on several occasions and apart from that all the paper staff knew I was going. I had to refuse another invitation, damned good one, too. I knew the ball would be as boring as hell and I'd know no one there."

"Did you mention that fact to anyone?"

"Yes."

"Then it's obvious. The papers were all egging Blackshirt on. He must have been looking round for someone like you who was going but wasn't well known. Don't you see, the person you told all that to is Blackshirt."

"Funnily enough that's what the police think," Lancy replied with heavy sarcasm. But it rolled off the reporter's back.

"Then they have their suspicions? Who is it?"

"They don't know and I don't know, for the simple reason I can't remember who it was I was speaking to! " "You can't remember?"

"No, I can't. All I know is that there was a group of people — that's right it was a dinner, I've suddenly come to. Where on earth could it have been?"

The reporter leaned forward excitedly. "Here's your chance! Five hundred quid! "

Lancy was thinking hard, but only to relieve his own ego. The police had been irate at his bad memory, and so was he, as normally he could truthfully boast about its excellence and accuracy. His brow creased. Then, "That's a washout, anyway. I've remembered but a fat lot of good it is."

"Who? It doesn't matter how imp— "

"It was at my club. And you might as well suspect the local parson! "

Jameson was almost frantic with rage and impatience. "What club and who was it?"

"The Junior Arts. And there were six or seven present. But since I know them all one way or another, it must have been some other occasion."

"It must have been one of those. Who was there?"

"First you suggest I know Blackshirt personally, then that he belongs to my club. Next thing you'll be saying I'm he! " said Lancy scornfully.

Jameson called for two more drinks and controlled his hasty temper with an effort. "All right, so they're out of the question — but just who was there?"

"Oakley. You know him. Maybe you think he's your man? Bradley of the *Evening Herald*. James the author, but since he's just come back from Scotland and was up there when all this happened I don't think even you could start imagining things. The rest of them I don't know — never met them before in my life. Oh yes! I remember one more. Verrell the novelist. You can sort that lot out for all I care, I'm going back to sleep."

Jameson glanced up with a crafty look. "It might be better if you didn't mention your return of memory to the police — after all, if Blackshirt is one of these men they will grab him and bang goes our reward. If you don't say a thing we stand a good chance of making it."

"I've no intention of telling anyone. As far as I'm concerned, if I never hear of this damned cracksman again, that will be too soon." He left, glad to get away.

*

Richard Verrell was feeling good. His new book was coming along well, and that morning he had received a cheque for accumulated royalties which was unusually heavy. But perhaps more than anything else, he enjoyed reading about himself in the papers. Journalism had given way to wild imagination, and since he knew the truth the result was ludicrous. There was only one cloud on the horizon — he still had no lead on the Darthweight pearls, or Janet.

The sun was shining and for once London seemed to possess a little beauty. He decided to go for a walk before starting work. Choosing a well-worn stick, Verrell let himself out of the front door, and strode quickly along the pavement in the direction of the park. From across the road Jameson watched with sharp eyes.

The reporter was not one to see money go a-begging. For three days he had been investigating what details he could discover regarding the men Lancy had mentioned — Verrell was the last one on the list. Not one of the others could possibly have been Blackshirt owing to various facts which Jameson had checked up on. The editor was getting annoyed and demanding action. If Jameson didn't hurry up and produce something he'd be shot off the present assignment — with the attendant loss of prospects regarding one thousand pounds. Dismally he flipped the finished cigarette into the gutter and walked across the road.

Roberts answered the door.

"Is Mr. Verrell in?"

"I'm afraid not, sir, he's just this moment gone out."

"Pity, still maybe you can tell me… I seem to know your face. Where the heck have I met you before?" Jameson stared intently at the other.

"I couldn't say, sir."

"Half a sec. Old Bailey, that's it. Only your name probably wasn't the same then as it is now. I was a junior reporter. What was it, larceny or burglary?" He sneered.

"I'm afraid I don't understand what you're talking about, sir."

"Not much you don't! You can change your name but you can't change your ruddy past… What the devil was it?" Suddenly he clicked his fingers. "Walker, that's who you are. 'Shifty' Jim Walker who did something like five years for safe-breaking."

Roberts shivered. It was a long time ago that he had been known by that name, and since he had turned straight. But the mention made him feel sick in the pit of his stomach.

"Just what are you doing here, my lad?" His voice was sharp.

"I'm Mr. Verrell's valet."

"Going up in the world. Look here, Walker "

"Roberts," said the other in a low voice.

"Roberts then, there're one or two things I want to know. I'm writing a series of articles on famous authors so just answer a few questions about Verrell."

"I regret to say I can tell you very little. Perhaps you will come back later and see Mr. Verrell personally." Roberts had recovered his normal composure.

"Just nark that and come across with what I want to know. Else your boss will be getting a visit from someone who can tell him a few facts that might astonish him I " Although Roberts's voice remained even, the tone made Jameson curse. "Mr. Verrell is already aware of the facts to which you have referred."

If Verrell knew he was a crook maybe he had a reason for employing him, thought Jameson. It was probably because such a person could be useful — to Blackshirt. An ex-crook in the house of a suspect; talk about birds of a feather!

When Jameson found there was nothing to be gained by blustering, his manner changed to one of heavy friendship. He pulled out a pocket-book and took out two one-pound notes which he crinkled between his fingers. "Don't take any notice of that — good heavens, man, I'm not the one who'd bust in to upset a man who'd turned over. Live and let live, that's my motto. But getting back to this article I've got to write. There's a couple of quid in it for you."

Jameson mistook the light in Roberts's eyes for cupidity and his silence for acceptance.

"Just tell me what his hobbies are, and how many books he's written, all that sort of guff."

"I really know very little about him."

Jameson took out another pound note. "Where does he go for his holidays? Does he prefer the wireless to television?" "Am I to understand that if I answer I…" Roberts indicated the money.

"Damn it, man, that's what I've been trying to tell you. Not much wonder you get pinched if you're that dumb! Now then, let's have it."

Roberts answered. Unfortunately he did not tell the truth, and Verrell would have had difficulty in recognizing himself.

"Just one more question," said Jameson, and, though he did not realize it, his voice had grown excited. "Where was Verrell Thursday night?"

Roberts looked at the money the other was holding. With bad grace Jameson handed it over.

"Thursday evening," repeated Roberts, his brow creased in thought. "Yes, I remember it was rather unusual."

"Go on," the reporter shouted.

"On Thursday evening Mr. Verrell was in his check suit. Most unusual, he usually wears his grey of an evening! "

Unceremoniously Roberts ushered the other through the door and shut it.

*

When Verrell returned half an hour later, exhilarated by the exercise, he was met by Roberts, who in quick and precise sentences repeated the gist of the interview with Jameson.

As Verrell moved into the sitting-room his brow creased in thought. The inference was only too obvious — a reporter from the *Daily Star*, the paper that was featuring his escapades, had for some reason become suspicious of him and was beginning to connect the name Verrell with the name Blackshirt. But how could the man have obtained that lead? There was only one source, and that would be through Lancy. Then, in all probability, both Lancy and the reporter had their suspicions — Verrell smiled wryly. Life was becoming complicated and exciting!

There was a ring at the front door, and he heard his valet's soft footsteps moving across the floor. Was this the police, with similar questions? A smooth-tongued inspector who would be extremely polite in the presence of a well-known author, and extremely searching since he might be in the presence of an equally famous cracksman?

"Miss Janet Dove," announced Roberts. Janet walked in, looking as neat and attractive as ever.

Chapter Nine

"Hallo, Richard, you can't think how pleased I am to see you again!"

"You!" Verrell's voice reflected his amazement. He knew she had more than her share of nerve and confidence, but he was surprised that she should deliberately seek him out. She must have realized that he would try to trace her for the sole purpose of regaining the pearls. The impudent gleam in Janet's eyes showed she guessed what he was thinking.

"Richard, that's not the way to greet a very old friend! I haven't seen you for days and days, and I've wanted to so much; then, when I finally screw up my courage, that's all you have to say."

"What — what on earth?" he mumbled.

"What am I doing here? I've come to ask you an important question, that only you can answer. And also to make you two propositions, one of which is that you lake me out to dinner tonight. I'm bored! "

"How the deuce you dare to come here after — after double-crossing me for a second time!"

"Richard dear, if I hadn't done it first, you'd have double-crossed me, wouldn't you? And it's not so long ago that you took advantage of my helpless position! Really, if you're still annoyed it shows you're not much of a sport! You had all the fun of doing the work you like so much, and then you had, or should have had, the pleasure of knowing that you helped me considerably. In any case, you must admit I was clever."

There was only one possible answer for Verrell to make. He roared with laughter. Never before had he met a girl he liked so much. She was charming and attractive and, though unscrupulous, so provocative in her sheer effrontery that despite everything Verrell knew he was glad to see her again.

But honour must be satisfied! "Look here, young lady, if you think I'm going to answer a single one of your questions, or listen to any proposition that you may make…" He tried to be stern.

"Don't be so stuffy. You'll be delighted when you hear what they are! Before I start, would you care to offer me a cigarette?"

"I'm sorry, Janet." Verrell quickly offered his case.

"Richard, you really are the most charming man I've ever met. Why don't you get married? Good heavens, even the thought makes him go red in the face! I'm getting too old for gadding round; how about settling down with me and raising a brood of little burglars?" Janet giggled as she saw Verrell's embarrassment. "Seriously, are you going to take me out to dinner?"

"I shall be charmed," he replied formally, having regained some measure of composure.

"Thank you. The next thing is: Do you know of a reliable fence? Somebody who will not try and diddle me?"

"Diddle *you*!" laughed Verrell.

"I'm in a bit of a quandary. I was aiming to clear out of the country as soon as I'd got the pearls. I could have sold them to the same person as before, and, provided I kept away from the roulette table, wouldn't have had to worry for a long time to come. But that wretch Peebles pinched my passport and I can't move! The Foreign Office are being extremely sticky about issuing another. They seem to take weeks to make up their mind. And I'm so short of money I had to sacrifice part of my wardrobe to pay the hotel bill. I've just got to lay my hands on something solid quickly — and the only person I could think of who would help me was you," she pleaded.

"So it all boils down to the fact that you want me to find the best market for the pearls which I went to all that trouble to obtain?" Verrell's voice was ironic.

"I suppose it does sound a little…" She paused and then continued more cheerfully, "But of course we go halves in whatever you can obtain — that was the second proposition I wanted to put to you."

Verrell's mind worked quickly. There seemed to be nothing wrong with what she said, yet he could not believe Janet would give up a half share so easily. Nevertheless, if she were really in such sorry straits, maybe the present solution was the only one of which she could think. As Blackshirt, he knew the biggest fence in London. Since his identity was unknown, he was always able to get a moderately reasonable price for such jewellery as he took along — for he was able to bargain with the sure knowledge that he could not be given away by the fence. But would Janet keep her side of the bargain, or had she already laid her plans for keeping the whole of the proceeds?

"I think it might be possible, Janet. If you let me have them I can take them along and ask a man I know what they are worth.'

91

"I'm sorry, Richard, but I'd rather keep them — if you lost them you'd feel so badly about it, wouldn't you, when it came to explaining to me? He'll know what they are like, since they are so well known." She spoke as though she really believed what she was saying.

"How about some lunch, then a show?" suggested Verrell, abruptly changing the conversation. Very cheerfully Janet agreed.

The day was fine and they decided to walk. Half-way to the restaurant Janet slipped her hand under Verrell's arm.

"Keep walking, Richard, but do you know anything about a dark-haired, rather oily-looking man of medium height, and not over well-dressed?"

"No, why?"

"Because a man answering to that description has been almost exactly thirty yards behind us since we left your flat."

Verrell recalled Robert's description of the journalist who had asked such disquieting questions. The valet had stressed a certain oiliness about the man. The presence of the snooper meant danger with a capital D. So he was still suspicious, this unknown!

Verrell's eyes gleamed with amusement. The man wouldn't learn much on this occasion!

*

Jameson had been given a free hand, and to some extent a free expense sheet, on one condition — that he bring Blackshirt to justice promptly. The editor had complimented him on his descriptions of the daring burglaries; but flatly stated that results were now demanded by the proprietor. News was slack, and nobody of any consequence was providing those 'hot' items which kept their reading-public amused and shocked.

Therefore the *Daily Star* must capture the criminal. It could then spend at least a week extolling its own brilliance in bringing the cracksman to justice.

Jameson, convinced that he had been clever enough to discover Blackshirt's identity, had set himself the task of following Verrell wherever he went. Sooner or later, he would surprise the cracksman during one of his night escapades, turn him over to the police, and then go back to the office and write it up.

The practice, he found, was not so simple. Standing in one section of a street, as inconspicuously as possible, for hours at a time was extremely tiring and boring. The two occasions when he had followed Verrell had proved only one thing… the author walked far too much by modern standards! Hence, after having escorted Janet and Verrell to the restaurant, a matinee, and another restaurant, Jameson decided to give up and to concentrate on night-time only, when it was far more likely that Blackshirt would appear.

When Verrell left his flat at ten the next evening, immaculate in evening dress, the reporter followed him to the Junior Arts Club. Since his quarry was remaining, apparently for the rest of the evening, Jameson returned home, where he pondered deeply, trying to see if there were a weak link in his chain of reasoning.

Verrell walked through the lounge, stopped to chat with a couple of friends, and then carried on straight out of the back entrance of the club. As he had reckoned, the reporter had a lot to learn about shadowing!

*

Otto Speyer ran a pawnbroker's shop, in which could be found an unlimited supply of junk. His living-rooms were directly above the shop, and it was from here that the majority of his business was conducted — after dark. He was the biggest fence in London and made a fortune buying stolen jewellery from thieves at pitiably low prices, secure in the knowledge that he held the whip-hand. He then sold the jewellery at considerable profit through channels he had formed in the many years he had been in that lucrative business. Crooks might curse him harshly when the price he offered was only a fiftieth of the value of the article in question, but they had to accept or starve. And it was bad policy not to sell to Mr. Otto once the original offer had been made; because at least two people had suddenly been arrested by the police just after precisely that had happened. And though no one liked to say anything definite...!

However, there was one man who neither feared, nor had cause to fear, the fence — Blackshirt. Appearing unannounced, in the early hours of the morning when it was sometimes necessary to awaken the sleeping man, and wearing his famous Blackshirt clothes, he drove hard bargains.

Peering over a table on which lay two diamond brooches, Otto laughed softly. He had paid two hundred for them and if he did not clear fifteen hundred, his name wasn't...

"I rather like those!"

Startled, the man swung round on his chair.

"Blackshirt! Why can't you come in like a normal human being, instead of making me jump from fright?" he asked plaintively. "Still, boys will be boys." He rubbed his hands together. Speyer always felt nervous and uncertain in the other's presence. For one thing, although Blackshirt never used force, there was a strong hint of steel beneath the smooth exterior. Secondly, he was the one person who could 'shop' Speyer without fear — which placed transactions on too level a plane!

"Good evening, Otto." Blackshirt bowed mockingly. "Where did you get those? Very nice indeed!"

Speyer hastily pushed the brooches into a leather bag, and returned them to a drawer. "A mere nothing, my friend, far beneath your notice. Now, what have *you* got for me this time?"

"The Darthweight pearls, Otto."

"I read about them. It was very clever of you, but they're too well known for me to handle — much too well known."

"I want forty thousand pounds." Blackshirt knew his man.

"Aah!" The fence gestured hopelessly. "Forty thousand I What do you think I am, a philanthropic society? Why, I *very* much doubt if I could get ten for them."

The argument was long. Both men knew to a few pounds where the deciding price would rest, but both refused to be hurried there. At last, however, it was settled.

"Now, my dear Blackshirt, we must have a drink! Always I have wanted to see the Darthweight pearls — to feel them! Ach, there's nothing like a pearl for beauty and warmth. Let me have them quickly, that I may fondle the wonderful gems."

"I haven't got them with me."

"You never trust me," sighed Speyer sadly. "Well, never mind, have some champagne with me to celebrate."

"No thanks."

"You think I put some arsenic in it?"

Blackshirt laughed by way of reply; then he spoke again and his voice hardened. "Now listen to me carefully, Otto. I shall not be bringing the pearls to you personally, for reason's best known to myself. Instead, a young lady will bring them. You are to pay her half of the price we agreed upon, and keep the other half for me. Never mind what she says, or what she does, only give her half."

"Are you afraid she's going to twist you?" chuckled Speyer.

"Just leave that end of it to me. I am telling you what you have to do. And if I were you, I wouldn't fail." There was a snap in Blackshirt's voice which caused the other to wince.

"My dear Blackshirt, as if I would."

Once safely home, Verrell undressed, bathed and donned pyjamas and dressing-gown. Then, stretching out in the most comfortable arm-chair, he lit a cigarette and inhaled deeply. Perhaps he was a fool, even now, to go halves with Janet! A little judicious fixing with the wily Otto, and he might have arranged to keep everything — but that would have gone against the grain. A thief he might be — but, paradoxically, a thief with far more honour than many a respected and prominent citizen. Possibly he could afford it since his writing kept him in comfort, if not luxury, and his night escapades were in the nature of a drug to satisfy his craving for excitement.

From Janet, his mind wandered until it tackled the problem of Jameson — one that could easily prove serious, if not fatal, should the reporter be lucky enough to stumble on some vital piece of evidence. Jameson must be shown that Verrell and Blackshirt were not one and the same person — that such a supposition was fantastic. Exactly how this was to be done was far from clear. Short of force, which he would under no circumstances use since it would have to be fatal, there seemed to be no effective way of removing the nuisance. That was, unless... He lit another cigarette as he explored the new possibility. He judged Jameson as a vain and boastful character, one who would want all the credit for success and be unwilling to share a fraction of the publicity, or the reward. If that were so, and if...

The ash-tray was full before he went to bed.

Chapter Ten

Peebles was not in a good temper. Of late nothing had gone right, and the final blow to his self-esteem and pocket had been the discovery that the pearls were false. That Blackshirt should have switched them over, and then have lost to Janet, only enraged him the more. Jim and Harry learned to their cost to keep away from him in the succeeding days.

He had had a market lined up for the fabulous Darthweight gems, a collector who was unorthodox in the extreme and paid good prices with no questions asked for any really choice pieces.

Jim, Harry and he had been searching London, visiting every fence they knew, trying to obtain a lead to Janet. Every effort had ended in a blank. No one had known a thing about her. Not one of the fences would admit he had been approached with regard to the pearls. As a last resort Peebles had approached Blackshirt, certain that if the other had met Janet he would say so. But even that idea had come to nought.

As if to prove him wrong, Verrell entered the room.

"Good morning, Peebles."

"Hallo, Verrell. What's yours?" When their respective interests did not conflict, there was a strange bond between the two men. Neither would deliberately betray the other, and each respected the capabilities of his opponent.

"A very dry Martini, please. Not a bad little place you have here. Quite cosy, in fact."

"No thanks to you if we manage to hang on to it. They're kicking up about the rent, which is a bit overdue. You wouldn't like to lend me a couple of thousand, would you?"

"No," replied Verrell, smiling.

"I thought not! Yet you're the cause of all my trouble. But for your wretched interference I'd be at the Savoy. What brings you here, anyway?" As he remembered his grievance he became annoyed.

"I've met Janet."

"What!" Peebles bellowed. Jim came hurrying into the room to see what the trouble was. At the sight of Verrell he whipped an automatic out of his pocket and levelled it. The enraged Peebles aimed a cushion that Jim missed only by moving hurriedly to one side.

"Get out! "

"But — you called "

"Get out before I…" Jim had already shut the door behind him.

"Where? When? What happened? Has she still got them?" Peebles spoke quickly, his eyes lighting up at the welcome news.

"She's still got them — and she's short of money."

"How do you know? Blackshirt, we'll get our own back now. We'll get those pearls if it takes us weeks 1 She's double-crossed us once too often. Got no more morals than the man in the moon I What's so funny about that?"

"Nothing." Verrell smiled broadly at the thought of a high-minded Peebles.

"What's she doing with them? How can we get them?"

"That's just what I've come to explain. Janet is willing to trade half their value in return for her passport. She's had an offer which she's decided to accept as she wants to get to the Continent in a hurry — it will take too long to get a new passport. She's bringing the chap along and he'll hand over the agreed price when we're all together."

Verrell could almost follow the working of Peebles' mind. Janet was bringing the pearls along — that was where they would return to their rightful 'owner'!

"There was one other thing. Both you and I must turn up alone. She doesn't trust you when you're with Jim and Harry. Said it was no good your trying to hide them somewhere handy as she'd be keeping careful watch!"

Peebles swore. Still, if he couldn't work the oracle on his own account against a man who never carried a weapon of any description, a woman, and some fence — then his name wasn't Peebles!

"How does the suggestion strike you?"

"Damned if I like taking a cut, but I suppose I'll have to," he replied sourly. "Have you made any arrangements with her?"

"Yes. Provided you're agreeable, we have arranged a meeting-place. Off Newark Road there are some large houses, one of which is owned by the Longton family. They're all away on holiday, and not due back for a month. Janet suggests we meet there in four days' time to settle the business. On the second floor is a small sitting-room which has only one window looking out on to the back of another house.

We make our way there independently to arrive at ten in the evening."

"Seems a damned complicated way of dividing a few pearls," grumbled Peebles, satisfied nevertheless, since in a secluded spot like that he would be able to carry out his plans.

"You know what women are!"

Shortly after, Verrell left, having omitted to mention one or two details which Peebles might have found somewhat interesting! In the first place he had been using Janet's name in vain, since it was hardly likely she had ever heard of the Longtons. Secondly, he had been invited to a party five houses along the road to be given by a Mrs. Sharp, in celebration of the coming-of-age of her youngest daughter. He had been asked to propose the health of the daughter, and, since the Press would be present, his presence during the evening would undoubtedly be recorded.

Jameson, judging by his continued appearance at odd hours outside the flat, was still suspicious. What greater proof of the complete fallacy of his theory could there be than a burglary committed by Blackshirt while Richard Verrell was attending a party nearby? The reporter would follow Verrell to the immediate neighbourhood of Newark Road, and his attention would then be drawn to the empty house. Inside he would meet Peebles, who's build, even when masked, could not be confused with that of Verrell. Thus confronted, Jameson could be quietly put to sleep by Blackshirt, acting from the rear. Peebles would be left convinced that Janet had no intention of turning up and had tried to trap him for reasons best known to herself — undoubtedly he would leave in a bad temper. Janet might be called to account if she ever met the Jackdaw again, but a few words would soon apportion the blame where it belonged. In the meantime Verrell would, having disposed of the reporter, suggest to the Jackdaw that they leave immediately, and so be able to return to the party in time to make his speech at ten-thirty. The plan seemed fool proof. There was just one difficulty — the Jackdaw did not dress in Blackshirt's clothes. He was always in the most nondescript garments, chosen deliberately.

But what if a black shirt were thrown casually on the floor, as though the owner had just taken it off? Surely that would be sufficient to prove to the reporter he was facing the redoubtable Blackshirt.

Gaily, Verrell made his way home, whistling a doubtful air from *La Traviata*.

As had been arranged, Verrell escorted Janet to a dinner-dance that evening, first for the pleasure of her company which was at all times very real, and secondly that he might tell her the result of his visit to Otto

Speyer. After several dances the couple sat down, and the waiter served the wine.

Janet leaned forward. "Richard, don't keep me in suspense any longer — what did he say?"

"Settled at twenty-nine thousand five hundred."

She sighed contentedly; her financial worries were at an end. "When can I collect it — what a wonderful thought that at last I shan't have to worry about each shilling I spend."

"I told Otto we would both be along in two days' time." Janet frowned.

"Is it really necessary for us both to go — I mean he might be watched by the police, for all we know, and if you were caught through me I'd never forgive myself. Richard, let me go alone, just in case. I can contact you immediately afterwards." She leaned forward, her face creased with worry, an unshed tear glistened in her eye at the thought of her partner in the hands of the police.

The waiter interrupted them as he deftly served the *hors-d'oeuvre*, then retired. Verrell hastily looked away. For a moment he had almost believed that she *would* meet him after she had seen Otto!

"Well, Richard?"

"I will have to let you know, Janet. I told him we would both come along; he would be suspicious if you go by yourself. But if you'd rather, I will see what I can do."

Quickly, Janet changed the conversation, not wishing to press the question too far. Really, the man whom the papers termed the arch-criminal Blackshirt was one of the most pliable males she had ever met. He was so courteous that he would not allow himself to doubt a woman's word, even for a moment — despite what had gone before."

Hardened as she was, unscrupulous and, where needs be, vicious, yet she had a whole-hearted admiration for this man who by sheer drive had risen from the dregs of the criminal fraternity.

Janet leaned forward. "Richard, I really am terribly glad you've taken me out tonight."

There was a look in her eyes that sent his blood racing and made him feel like singing — though he doubted that the band would appreciate his efforts!

*

By the night of the party at the Sharps' house, Jameson was feeling depressed. Only a few days ago he had been so certain, so sure of himself

— and now he was almost ready to confess he had been wrong. His editor had not helped. The man was friendly enough when things were going well. But only yesterday Jameson had been called in to report his progress. Since his account added up to precisely nothing, the editor had tactfully assured the reporter that there were dozens of men ready to take over his job. For three days more he might be allowed to waste the time and money of the *Daily Star* and then...

Three short days in which to discover the identity of Blackshirt, provide a front-page story and boost the sales. And to date, all he could find to do was to wait for hours on end outside a flat. True, the circumstantial evidence was strong, but heaven knows, circumstantial evidence was not infallible.

At that moment the reporter stiffened. Excitement formed a knot in his stomach. Coming out of the flat opposite was Richard Verrell — moving as he had never done before. Instead of his immaculate evening coat, he was wearing a darkish raincoat which even at a distance showed distinct signs of wear. A black slouch hat was pulled well over his forehead, and successfully concealed the major part of his face. He did not walk briskly out on to the pavement as was usual, but gave a quick glance up and down the road before he furtively, or so it seemed to the reporter, slipped out and joined the thin stream of passers-by. Then, a conclusive piece of evidence to Jameson, he noticed that as Verrell walked there was no sharp 'crunch' of shoe-leather on the pavement, only a dull swish — his quarry was wearing crepe-soled shoes.

Forty yards behind Verrell, Jameson moved cautiously. He was not adept at shadowing, but at all costs he must raise no suspicions. At last he was about to prove his theory.

*

At the entrance to Newark Road, Verrell quickened his pace and disappeared round the corner. Taking his time, Jameson followed, and likewise turned. The street was well-lit and some six hundred yards long. But there was no sign of the man he had been following. He seemed *to* have been swallowed by the night. So Verrell the famous author and Blackshirt the audacious criminal *were* one and the same person! Somewhere along the road Blackshirt was about to break into a house. This time, however, he would not leave unassisted! Racing for the nearest phone booth, the reporter inserted two pennies and dialled a number. Hurriedly he gave a series of directions to the night editor of the *Daily Star* — which was one move Blackshirt had not reckoned on!

*

"Good evening, Jane."

"Good evening, Richard. I am so glad you've been able to come along; we don't see nearly enough of you these days. This is my youngest daughter, Moira."

"How do you do, Moira. I'm afraid I haven't seen you since you were at school; must be more than six years ago."

"And I wore pig-tails, I suppose?"

"I'm certain if you did they didn't make you any the less charming."

Moira laughed. His stilted speech made with humorous intent more than disarmed her annoyance at being reminded of her childhood. Just then two more guests were announced.

Before leaving her side, Verrell requested that she reserve a dance for him.

At a quarter to ten Verrell prepared to leave so that he might be back in time to make his speech at ten-thirty, but he was detained for five minutes when he met an old acquaintance who insisted on drinks and a discussion on the literary world in general; he was finally able to excuse himself on the plea of consulting his hostess on a point in his speech.

Having visited the house previously he knew the lay-out of the ground floor, and was able to reach the garden unseen. The garden, large for a London house, had a small gate at the end which opened on to a lane running the length of the row of buildings. It was seldom used save by the immediate households on either side. A short walk brought him level with the empty building. Making certain he was unseen Verrell removed the 'dicky' that contained white shirt, collar and tie, and carefully concealed them in a handy clump of grass. Straightening up, he drew on his hood and gloves and once again was dressed as Blackshirt. Having made sure he still had the spare black shirt, he climbed over the wall and merged into the shadows. Only the slightest of muffled squeaks indicated that he had opened a window.

Jameson, having successfully tracked Blackshirt to the scene of one of his crimes, realized with dismay that he did not know which house was being broken into! It might be any of the first twenty on either side, allowing for the time it had taken him to come up to the corner of the road. He cursed himself for having so cautiously kept at too great a distance.

Just then Jameson saw a flicker of light from a second-floor window a little farther on. It was gone almost before he could be certain he had seen it, but a few seconds later there was another flash. "He's so confident, he's careless," concluded the reporter as he mentally marked the building, little realizing that Blackshirt was calling him names for not acting more quickly. The band of helpers, who should have turned up within four minutes of the phone call, were still missing so the impatient reporter decided to leave a mark to guide them and enter the house alone.

He stuck his hat, extremely well-known at the office, on top of one of the spikes of the front gate. Then, drawing an automatic from his pocket, softly made his way up to the front door. It opened at his touch. The reporter heard a slight noise from upstairs which convinced him that whatever was happening, was taking place on the second floor. His mouth was dry, and his hand unsteady. Every time one of the uncarpeted stair-boards creaked at his passing he held himself in readiness to run.

Blackshirt had already spoken to the Jackdaw. After a pleasant but mistrustful greeting on either side, he had laid his spare garment down on the table. Peebles was curious, but seemed satisfied at the mumbled explanation that it was some whim of Janet's. He was solely concerned with his own problem.

"She's late," muttered Blackshirt. "I'll go and see if I can find out what's happened."

"Women always are," grumbled the Jackdaw, at the retreating form which disappeared with uncanny speed as soon as it was beyond the range of the shaded light.

Blackshirt, motionless in the far recess of the landing, watched the reporter stealthily make his way upstairs until he was outside the room from which a chink of light escaped. Blackshirt could have stretched forward a hand and touched him.

Jameson was uncertain what to do. He knew that he should wait until his friends turned up before attempting anything — but if he captured the cracksman single-handed then his would be the greater glory. Slowly he eased the catch of the door until he was certain it was free^ — then thrust the door open, and stared at the man who sat at his ease smoking a cigarette, his black shirt handy on the tabte — so this was Blackshirt! By no stretch of imagination could it be Verrell, so dissimilar the build.

Behind the reporter Blackshirt was poised, in his hand a chloroform pad. The next second he would have applied it when suddenly the front door of the house was thrown open. Cries of 'Jameson' echoed up the stairs. The sudden noise distracted Blackshirt and for a moment he remained motionless summing up the approaching danger.

Without looking up Peebles said, "What the hell's the row, Blackshirt?" As he rose from the chair he saw the reporter for the first time.

Blackshirt felt stunned. By one second's inattention his whole scheme was ruined. The reporter had heard enough to realize that it was not Blackshirt before him. Then events moved too fast for inquests.

Jameson half turned and from the corner of his eye caught sight of a black shadow. There was Blackshirt, scant inches away from him I Awkwardly he tried to swivel his automatic round. Blackshirt saw the movement and brought his right hand up hard, but at the last moment the reporter moved his chin. The blow landed on his neck, left him sick and dizzy, but still conscious. "Up here," he cried. "Blackshirt's…" This time there was no mistake. Jameson crumpled up and lay still.

Up the stairs came a yelling mob. Five of the largest and strongest of the newspaper's staff, and as the foremost caught sight of the unconscious Jameson, and Blackshirt moving away from him, he redoubled his speed. In the doorway Blackshirt caught the leading man, a red-nosed individual, a blow to the body that doubled him up, but the blond, curly-headed man behind threw himself forward and caught the cracksman round the middle, bringing him to the ground. Someone aimed a savage kick, and though Blackshirt managed to roll aside, the toe of the boot caught him a glancing, agonizing blow. Hands reached for his hood. Twisting and heaving he dragged himself to his knees, then by a supreme effort upright. Across the room he saw Peebles struggling, savagely trying to get to his pocket where he had his automatic.

The man behind Blackshirt was trying to throttle him with an arm lock. Curly-head panted as he struggled to hold his hands down. Red-nose was picking himself up slowly… if he joined in Blackshirt was lost. He threw his weight forward. The man behind countered the movement and increased the leverage of the lock until Blackshirt could only draw a wheezing gasp of air into his strained lungs, whilst he concentrated every ounce of his strength in breaking his arms free. Back and forth they stamped, the dust rising in clouds which stung the eyes. Then he had one arm free. Again he threw his weight forward, again the others countered. With his free hand he caught hold of the curly hair and threw himself backwards. As the weight shifted, the man behind was caught off balance.

The whole group fell. As they did so Blackshirt brought his foot into Curly's stomach and thrust upwards — the man was flung backwards, hit the wall and collapsed. Beneath him Blackshirt heard the other grunt with pain, at the same time the stranglehold relaxed and he was able to gasp in a lungful of air.

Peebles was reeling dizzily. One of his assailants had a leather cosh, and with it he had caught the Jackdaw across the back of the head, drawing blood. Blackshirt lunged forward, caught the man in the back and sent him flat on the floor. He turned and, parrying a blow with his left, he countered with his right, which landed flush on the fifth man's jaw.

Red-nose and Curly had recovered and this time they came in warily. Behind him was a chair. He picked it up and threw it. It smashed into pieces as it felled Red-nose. As Blackshirt moved forward his left foot was caught and pulled backwards. He fell, cracked his head on the floor, and for a moment all was black. Pain came in waves. Hands once more clutched him, hammered at him. Another vicious kick to his side made him gasp. Every nerve in his body was jangling, instinct alone kept him fighting.

He lashed out with his right foot; it caught someone on the shin. He jerked his knee up and a man groaned. A blow caught him on the side of his head, another under the heart. Then he in turn struck blindly home. Jameson, who had recovered, came in groggily clutching a heavy paperweight. He smashed at Blackshirt's right arm and paralysed it. Throwing out left-hand punches as quickly as he was able, Blackshirt held them at bay for a few seconds, but the numbers were too great. In a huge ball of flying arms and legs they once more crashed to the ground.

Just then the Jackdaw fired. The man with the cosh dropped it and clapped his left hand to his shoulder. The fight stopped as quickly as it had started, with two of the men on the floor, still unconscious.

"Damn you," snarled the Jackdaw, drawing a handkerchief across his wound. "Get up against that wall. I'll kill the first one who moves."

Sullenly the men shuffled across until they came up against the far wall. At a savage command from Peebles they crossed their hands above their heads.

"Come on, Blackshirt, leave those… to look after themselves."

Blackshirt rose from the two unconscious forms, satisfied that neither was seriously hurt. Together they backed towards the door.

"Get this," swore Peebles, "if one of you moves a finger before we're clear of this house, I'll empty the magazine at the lot of you."

The depleted staff of the *Daily Star* stood rigid long afterwards.

*

Mrs. Sharp was becoming worried. It was time for Verrell to propose the toast, but he was not to be found. She was on the point of asking someone else to take over when he came up to her.

"Forgive me, Jane, I was feeling a trifle off colour, so I went outside for a breath of fresh air. Ronald came up and told me you were in the dickens of a flap."

"Ronald is an irreverent young man. Are you feeling better now?" she asked in a worried tone.

"Fine, thanks."

"What have you been doing? You've got a bruise on the side of your face the size of a half-crown."

"I've been fighting," he replied with an impudent grin.

Grimly she took his arm. "You *will* be fighting if you don't hurry up and do your duty I "

Chapter Eleven

The next morning the editor of the *Daily Star* was 'requested' to see the chairman.

Sir Arnold Bernborough was a majority shareholder, and to all intents and purposes ran the paper. In his drive to increase the circulation he had successfully lowered the previous low standard of the paper. The *Daily Star* catered for those who liked their news as sensational as possible and as spicy as possible.

The editor knocked at the glass-fronted door. A scared secretary answered. "Will you come along, Crowson? He'll see you right away."

"What's he like?" he asked nervously.

The secretary shrugged his shoulders. Crowson bit his lips.

"Come in! I've been waiting half an hour for you. Didn't anyone tell you I wanted to see you?"

"Yes, Sir Arnold, I came as soon as "

"Have you seen the papers this morning?"

"Yes, sir," he answered miserably.

"Then you've read what they've got to say about the *Star* and me. Have you?" The chairman paced the floor, his heavy face scowling. Every now and then he thumped a clenched fist into his hand for greater emphasis. "Have you read the *Sun*?"

"No — no, sir."

"Here you are. Front page. Read it, man."

Sir Arnold sat down behind his desk. "Read where it says 'everybody connected with the *Daily Star* is to be complimented on the way they bungled the whole affair'. Headlines of the *Daily Guardian*: 'The *Star* bungles arrest of Blackshirt.' " He crumpled up two more papers on the desk and threw them at the waste-paper basket.

Crowson maintained a discreet silence.

"We've been made to look a pack of idiots. What the devil have you got to say about it?"

"I'm very sorry, Sir Arnold, but you said that the police "

"Never mind what I said. Why did this Blackshirt get away? What fool messed up the whole affair and made a laughing-stock of the paper? Were you in charge?"

"I? No, sir I left everything to Jameson."

"What name — Jameson?"

The chairman called for the reporter over the intercom. Then he dismissed the editor.

"Are you Jameson?"

"Yes, sir."

"You're fired! Take a month's notice."

"What?" Sir Arnold regarded Jameson through half shut eyes.

"But why?"

"Why are you fired?"

"Yes, sir." He had expected a disagreeable interview, but had not been prepared for dismissal. Jameson was a single man, and he had always lived beyond his means. A reporter from the *Daily Star* had scant chance of securing a job with one of the reputable papers, and if Sir Arnold carried out his threat Jameson would be hard put to make a living.

"You have the nerve to stand there and ask *me* why you're fired? I'll tell you, young man. Because you've made me and the paper look the biggest fools on Fleet Street. That's why. Now get out."

"But, sir, it wasn't my fault, I — "

"Whose fault was it? Were you in charge?"

"Yes, sir, but the men from the staff didn't arrive on time." Jameson spoke as rapidly as he could form the words, determined not to let his employer speak until he had finished. "I went on ahead, and actually surprised Blackshirt — or the man I thought was Blackshirt. If the others had had the sense to leave a guard on the door downstairs, we'd have captured both men!"

"Are you trying to tell me that it wasn't your fault?"

"Yes — yes, sir."

"Stuff and nonsense. In any event you're still fired. Let that be a lesson to any other incompetent member of my staff." He impatiently signalled to the reporter to go.

Jameson was desperate. "Sir, if you'd only give me one more chance. I — I know who Blackshirt is."

"What's that?" snapped Sir Arnold, leaning forward. "You know him? Who is he?"

"I don't actually know him," stammered the reporter, "but I'm practically certain I know the identity of the cracksman."

"Who is it? I'll see he gets landed in gaol. Daring to make a fool of me!"

"I can't say, sir. I haven't any proof yet. But if you'd give me one..."

"I'll give you four days — after that out you go. I'll tell Crowson you have four days to establish the identity of Blackshirt. Send him in to me, right away."

Jameson left, grimly determined. If he didn't prove Verrell was Mr. Ruddy Blackshirt he'd be out of a job. God! How he hated that man. If it was the last thing he did, he'd see Blackshirt behind prison bars.

*

Otto Speyer grunted in annoyance as a cat yowled. His undercover job as a fence carried a considerable element of risk, but this he had, by good management, reduced to a minimum. Yet only two days ago a small-time thief had, in an endeavour to save his own skin, tried to incriminate Speyer. Warned by the criminal grape-vine, Otto had been prepared for the police search and the Nosy Parkers had drawn a blank. Nevertheless, it had emphasized the perpetual danger of his occupation.

"You seem deep in thought!" came a voice from the corner of the room. Blackshirt stepped into the view of the startled man.

"Blackshirt!" Speyer wiped his forehead. "Please to not always cause me to jump so when you arrive. Anyone else lets me know beforehand that I may prepare, but you just arrive 'whoosh'. Don't you know I have a weak and jumpy heart?"

"Sorry," grinned Blackshirt, not believing one word of what Speyer said.

"What have you got for me this time?"

"Nothing. I came to see what you have for me."

"Nothing," Speyer replied in a flat voice.

"Hasn't she seen you yet?"

"Yes; she's been — and gone."

"Where is the money, then?" Blackshirt's voice hardened dangerously. There was a snap to it that made even Speyer flinch.

"She wouldn't sell, Blackshirt."

"Wouldn't sell? What do you mean?"

"As soon as she heard that I would keep half the money for you, she refused to give me a single pearl. Even threatened me with a revolver. Please do not send another woman like her along."

"Where did she go? If I'd known, I would have followed her — I suppose you didn't?"

"Why should I?"

"Well, that's that!" After the slight burst of temper Blackshirt shrugged his shoulders in the realization there was nothing more he could do.

"But I know where she was going," artfully continued Speyer, after the pause.

"Where?" His interest quickened again.

"To 'Softy' Joe Calthorpe. She wanted the name of someone who would set a pearl different, with no questions asked."

"Why the deuce didn't you say so in the first place, you old ruffian?" laughed Blackshirt, amused at the roundabout way the other had taken to impart the news. "Where does 'Softy' live?"

"Near the docks. Lime Square, it's called. Past East Ham Underground, and it's down there somewhere — anyone will tell you. But don't go in that rig-out. Blackshirt isn't liked so hot down there."

"Thanks a lot, Otto."

Blackshirt disappeared the way he had come.

The next morning a rough sailor ambled along a road of shabby looking houses with the air of a man who had nothing to do until the pubs opened. He wore a filthy singlet, a pair of dungaree trousers, and an equally disreputable jacket, which occasionally he took off and carried over his arm. A hand-rolled cigarette drooped from his lips; the smoke curled up to his face and then away; every so often he loudly cleared his throat, and spat into the gutter. Altogether a far cry from Richard Verrell, the popular novelist.

Aimless as his walk appeared, he finally reached Lime Square, a neighbourhood that was, if anything, more evil and smelly than that he had already passed through.

Verrell loathed the few contacts he now had to have with the slum areas of London. All too vividly it brought back memories of his childhood, and the eternal question — who was he? Was he born in the gutter and merely stolen from such surroundings — impossible! Else why the memories of a nursemaid? Was he born of rich parents, who had spent days, months and years searching for him? Far more likely, if his innate appreciation of all that was beautiful counted for anything — added to the fact that he had not been content with the lot in which he found himself, but had battled against almost insurmountable odds.

"You ain't a type wot looks where 'e's going, is yer?" Verrell was brought back to his surroundings by sharp con tact with another man.

"Sorry, mate, finkin'."

"Finkin'! Gor blimey, wotever for?"

"Can't remember Softy's 'ome number; don't know it, does yer?"

"Wot yer want Softy for?"

"That's my business."

"All right, no 'arm meant. Over there. The one with a brass knocker, see. He..."

Verrell turned his shoulders on the loquacious guide, and crossed to the house. He knocked on the door and waited.

"Yus?"

"Softy?"

"Yus."

"Otto asked me to come 'ere."

"He did, did 'e. Wots yer name?"

"George Bullock."

"Where you from?"

"Up the river."

"All right, come in," Calthorpe said after he had summed up his visitor.

He led the way in to what seemed to be the living-room, belched abruptly, and pointed to a chair. Before he sat down, Verrell offered the other a cigarette from a torn, cheap packet.

"What you want, Bullock?"

"You can 'andle pearls, can't you?"

"Maybe yes; maybe no." The eyes became wary.

"Turn 'em into ear-rings, can't yer?"

" 'Tain't impossible."

"Ever done it afore, Softy?"

"What's that to do with you?" There was a vicious gleam in his eyes. He had a deep-rooted dislike of questions, and he had a strong suspicion that he might be dealing with a 'nark'.

"I ain't goin' to rat on you, Softy, don't think that! I ain't goin' to let on that you 'andled a little something the other day. Something wot ain't so far off pearls as it might be."

Softy Joe was amazed — and a little scared. He liked to keep his private trade very private. And here was someone who -seemed to know a great deal about it. His hand moved closer to his right pocket.

"Who told you, and what's it to you?"

"Just keep that hand of yours out of your pocket. I ain't meanin' no harm."

"Who told you, then?" He was still suspicious.

"I've been followin' that woman." Verrell's voice rose in anger. "She helped me to get them, but I did all the ruddy work. I stuck me head into trouble, then when I gives 'er the goods, she ups and runs! Gratitude! I found out where she got to, and then traced 'er here. I went to Otto, and asked him if he didn't know a little about you. Said maybe you sometimes played around with little bits of your own stuff, changing it for your old woman. A nod's as good as a wink to me, so I comes down 'ere to ask you what that woman has been up to. And I came to ask if this here might help your memory. When I gets to see her, she'll wish she didn't rat on me! " He pulled twenty dirty one-pound notes out of his top pocket. The avaricious gleam in the man's eyes did not escape Verrell.

"Took 'ere, George. I'll do you a good turn! She comes and wants two pearls, nice big 'uns, made into ear-rings. She pays me on the spot; and asks me to tell her nibs when they're ready."

"Have you finished 'em yet?"

" 'Old your horses. Yesterday I finished them and sent them off to an address she gives me, but it ain't no good your asking where 'cos it was a post office."

"You don't know where she is, then?"

" 'Old on, I keeps tellin' you. I asked 'er where she wanted to sell the ear-rings, and she says at a jeweller's. Then I says what one, and she wasn't goin' to tell me 'til I says each jeweller what is big enough to take pearls this big, and they was woppers, has a different sort of design they likes. So she comes out with the jeweller what she's takin* it to, so there you is."

"What was the name, Softy?"

He indicated the money and Verrell handed it over. Joe tested each one in turn. "The Royal Strand Jewellers, just off the Strand, chum, that's where she was off to."

With a muttered word of thanks, Verrell left the house and, as quickly as he dared, the neighbourhood.

*

Dressed once again in decent clothing, Verrell walked briskly along the Strand until he came to the large jewellery shop mentioned by 'Softy'.

Eagerly he scanned the windows, but nowhere could he see the pearl ear-rings he was trying to trace. In the short time he had handled the Darthweight pearls he had learned how superb was their texture — and he could see nothing comparable.

Verrell walked in and was met by an assistant, who sized up the potential customer.

"Good afternoon, sir. Can I help you?"

"I'm looking for a pair of really fine pearl ear-rings. Have you anything suitable?"

"Yes, sir, as it happens we have. This morning a French lady offered us a pair. She has been forced to sell her personal jewellery — very sad, sir, when this sort of thing happens! But these ear-rings are the most exquisite it has been our privilege to handle. Superb craftsmanship. Perhaps you would like to see them."

The assistant unlocked a glass show-case to the right of where Verrell was standing. He brought out a jewel case which he opened and laid on top of the glass. Verrell gasped with surprise. If anyone ever deserved a commendation for good work well done, it was 'Softy'. The ear-rings might have been genuine antiques. The pearls looked magnificent. It seemed impossible that they were not in their accustomed setting. Verrell had wondered how Janet could possibly succeed in selling pearls which had been so recently stolen and were so well known. Here was the answer.

"They are magnificent, aren't they, sir?"

"They certainly are. You know, it's funny, but I've a feeling I've seen them before!"

"Maybe you have met the Countess Kollinov, sir."

"Good lord, yes, I remember the name well! It was at Cannes two years ago, I think. Do you happen to know where she's staying?"

The assistant was not interested in the countess. "I'm afraid I don't, sir, but the manager might. We're asking two thousand guineas for these, sir. Quite reasonable for pearls so perfectly matched and of such fine texture. These earrings really are the most magnificent we have handled."

"I'm afraid that's rather more than I had in mind. I like them, but it is too much."

The assistant was disappointed. With superior condescension, he produced some of the other stock. After fifteen minutes Verrell declared himself uncertain, but announced that he would most certainly return.

"I would like to speak to the manager for a moment." "I'll see if he is free, sir."

The manager *was* free and soon appeared.

"Good afternoon, sir. I gather you wanted to see me about those pearls."

"No, it's not quite that. I wonder whether you could give me the owner's address, as I have just discovered she's by way of being an old friend of mine."

"I'm very sorry, sir. She asked me not to let anyone have it, since, as she finds herself in very straitened circumstances, she would rather not meet any former acquaintances. Naturally we have it, we are acting as agents with regard to the sale, but I'm sorry that I must refuse you, sir. I hope you'll understand."

"Certainly. There's one other question which perhaps you will be able to answer. I'm sorry if I am detaining you." "Not at all, sir."

"What type of safe would you recommend? I have some jewellery, or I should say my wife has, and at the moment it is locked in a casket which isn't very secure."

"Well, sir, we have two safes. That one," and the manager pointed to one corner where a very large safe stood open, "is an old 'Randax', installed when this place was first built. It's not a good one by modem standards, and we keep only our records in it. For our main stock we use an ultramodern 'Randax', which is guaranteed absolutely burglar-proof. One like ours would possibly be too large for your purpose, but they make them in all sizes."

"The old one would be twenty times too large for me, so I hesitate to think what your new one would do to my flat." Verrell laughed.

The manager politely did the same. "The old safe is far too large for us, sir, we don't use half the space; but it would cost too much to have it removed."

"Thanks a lot. Sorry to have troubled you."

"No trouble at all, sir."

Verrell walked happily out of the shop. A 'long shot' had prompted his questions with regard to the safe. He had recognized it for what it was the moment he had entered. But with the added information the manager had given him, a wild suggestion had occurred to him.

Chapter Twelve

The two counter-assistants at the Royal Strand Jewellers were worried. It was past three o'clock in the afternoon, and still the manager wandered between the shop and his office — to their annoyance since it was their invariable custom, completely contrary to a supposedly invariable house-rule, that each in turn should leave for a quick cup of tea at a shop just round the corner. But at last a series of cheerful gulps from behind a glass-fronted door enabled the first man to slip out of the shop.

Soon after the assistant had left a man walked in. Unmindful of the warm spring weather outside, he wore a dark mackintosh buttoned up to his neck, and a slouch hat pulled low across his forehead. The assistant was unimpressed; judging by his clothes the man had entered the wrong class of jewellers. But the sudden incisive snap of his voice, which carried an air of authority, made the assistant forget his supercilious manner.

"Where's the manager?"

"He's busy at the moment, sir."

"Tell him I want to see him."

"Would you mind informing me why you want to see him, sir? He is usually occupied at this time."

"Just tell him I want to see him at once. I am a police inspector and I want a word with him in private. Here's my card." The inspector presented a card, which he replaced before the other could take more than a cursory glance. "And hurry, the matter's important."

"I'm sorry, sir, but it's rather unusual for us to have a-

"Will you kindly hurry!"

"Yes, sir."

The assistant knocked at the manager's door.

"Yes, what is it?"

"Excuse me, sir, but a police inspector wants to see you at once; he's in front now."

"An inspector! What's gone wrong? Tell him I'll be right out." The manager hastily finished his tea, wiped his mouth with the back of his hand, and walked into the shop. The only person present was the assistant.

"Well, where is he?"

"I — I don't know, sir. He was here when I came in to see you, but when I returned he'd gone."

"Gone; gone where?"

"I don't know, sir."

"And where's Simpson? Is everybody disappearing?"

Just then the missing Simpson returned, coming to an abrupt halt when face to face with the manager.

"Where have you been?"

"I — I "

"So you left the shop, strictly against orders. Is it necessary..." The manager dwelt at some length on the penalty for disobeying orders, then suddenly remembered the missing C.I.D. officer. "Is anything missing, either of you? Check-up this instant! I must phone and see what they know about this affair. Take an inventory immediately. Oh, what if..." He was frantically dialling a number.

From the call the manager learned that no inspector had been detailed to call at his shop. With rising panic he helped his staff check the contents of the show-cases; to their relief and amazement, not a single piece appeared to be missing. The manager rang back the Yard, and informed them. After that he hurried to a small bottle he kept tucked behind some books; the liquid refreshment therein was very necessary to still his agitated heart.

Meanwhile Blackshirt was finding his quarters in the large Randax safe exceedingly cramped. As the assistant had rushed in to the manager, so Blackshirt had quickly entered the safe and settled down behind the stacks of papers, ledgers and documents. He was in a precarious position — to say the least. When they found he had disappeared, would they think of searching in the open safe, or would they be satisfied that he had left empty-handed? Would anyone have reason to search for some document or ledger, for if so he could not hope to escape detection. When they closed the shop, would anyone inspect the safe? Would there be sufficient air inside to last him the three hours before he dared break out — would the safe prove to be one that could be opened from the inside? Lastly, if he succeeded in discovering the information he wanted and in leaving the safe, how could he escape from the shop? There were so many unanswerable questions that he gave up trying to answer them, and lay back as comfortably as possible.

Behind his barricade of books he grew stiffer and stiffer, until each and every joint in his body ached. He dared not move lest he should disturb something and make a noise. Yet to remain where he was, motionless, became a painful torture. Enviously, he listened to the two assistants walking around.

Five o'clock approached and swift preparations were made to close up and leave. Show-cases were either emptied, or else securely locked. The manager dashed around giving flustered instructions. Finally, only one job remained.

"Put the books away, Simpson."

Footsteps approached the safe. Blackshirt braced himself for instant action should he be detected. But Simpson, somewhat untidily, merely threw the books inside, clanged the safe door to and locked it.

Blackshirt was imprisoned within walls of steel.

First, he permitted himself the luxury of stretching. For a time it was even more painful to move than it had been to remain still, but as the cramped limbs regained their normal circulation, the pain gradually eased.

He released the torch from the belt he wore next to his skin, and pressed the button. His first task was to find out whether he could escape from the safe! With a heartfelt sigh of relief he realized his gamble had come off. The safe was secured by a glorified type of the usual door lock. This was covered in with a heavy metal casing. But since the casing was secured by screws, a few minutes' work would enable him to tackle the locking mechanism direct. Some safes of similar type had an extra bar, secured independently outside, but in the short time he had been in the shop the first day he had been unable to see one.

The air inside would be sufficient to last him three to four hours, which would make it nine before he need finally leave the safe. The later the better, since then there would be fewer people about. Risking nothing, however, he fixed the torch so that its beam was directed on the lock, then, with a small screwdriver, he set to work to remove the casing.

In ten minutes the casing was off. Taking one of three skeleton keys that he had brought with him, he tried it in the lock. It would not turn the mechanism, but after he had tried all three, it proved a closer fit than the other two. With a small file he whittled away the edges. A second try, a few more adjusting strokes with the file, and the key turned. Switching off the torch, he pushed the safe door to make certain he could leave at will — but it remained immovable. Hastily he checked that the bolt had unlocked. There was only one explanation — there *was a* bar outside the safe!

It was serious since it would be necessary to knock a small panel out of the safe door to be able to work on the bar outside. It would take some time to drill in a circle the number of holes required before he could knock the panel of steel out — admittedly the holes would let in some air, but would the amount be sufficient to enable him to continue work? The air inside the safe would last three hours in normal conditions, but would scarcely do so once he began the heavy manual work of drilling. Everything depended on the speed with which he could drill, and the thickness of the steel.

He unbuckled the belt he wore round his body, laid it in a convenient spot, and selected a brace and bit. His tools were of necessity small, but what they lacked in size they made up for in quality. Of the finest steel obtainable, and where necessary diamond-tipped, it was seldom anything could resist them.

Time passed. Sweat poured off Blackshirt's brow as he drilled. In spite of the half circle of holes which he had already made the air was becoming heavy, forcing him to breathe more quickly than usual.

Three-quarters of the way round — and the act of turning the drill had become an almost impossible feat. Every muscle demanded rest, the sweet comfort of rest. His head began to throb.

With only two holes left to drill, he sank to the floor, gasping for air, hazy in mind as to what he was doing; why he was doing it. His only thought was sleep. But his disciplined will forced him to his feet again. With dull eyes he gazed before him. "Little holes," he mumbled stupidly. Then the drill was turning. Round and round, while he thought of green pastures with the sky above, reaching to infinity and containing so much fresh air it hurt to think of it. Another hole drilled. His fumbling fingers withdrew the drill. One more — one more what? — he didn't know, didn't care, wasn't interested. But again his hand was turning. Was he doomed to go on, like the Flying Dutchman, year after year turning his right hand in circles? Why couldn't he rest for a moment, then continue?

Another hole. The last. But one thing remained to be done; to knock the panel of iron out. His first blow hardly made a noise, the second none at all. Blackshirt let his aching hands fall to his side. His right hand brushed against something solid, a paper-weight, on top of a pile of dusty old files. Gripping it with both hands, he beat it against the safe door. There was a sharp crack, and the circle of metal fell on to the floor of the shop. Gasping, he thrust his nose and mouth against the opening, and gulped in the cool fresh air.

Within another quarter of an hour he had sawn through the bar, and was out of the safe that had so nearly cost him his life. Then, fully recovered, he adjusted his mask — and stepped back.

Half an hour's search through the various books and he discovered where Janet was staying. Newgate Hotel, Bayswater. 'That's that,' he thought, 'now for home I'

Curiously he looked into the show-cases to see what had been left there. While he would, since he was so handy, have liked to take a few of the choicer pieces from the main safe, he was perfectly willing to accept the manager's estimate of its toughness. Some months previously he had come up against a new Randax, and full of confidence had begun operations. Six hours later he had returned home, having hardly dented the modern processed steel.

The show-cases were filled with small pieces; diamond rings, opals, sapphires, all of no great value. Until the small pin-prick of light from Blackshirt's torch illuminated two pearls that he had seen before. For some reason the pearl ear-rings had been left out — maybe due to the haste in which everyone had gone home, after so much time had been spent in searching for the vanished inspector.

Five minutes later the Royal Strand Jewellers no longer possessed a superb pair of ear-rings belonging to the Countess Kollinov.

Blackshirt was then faced with the task of breaking *out* of the jewellers! During his preliminary investigation he had been dismayed to find that the small manager's office led only to a basement in which the other safe was situated. The three rooms, together with a small bathroom, proved to be a self-contained part of the building. He was left with only one mode of egress — through the front door.

The windows and doors of the shop were guarded by steel bars, the ones covering the windows being a fixed fitting. Inspecting the barrier over the door, he saw that it was held in place by a Yale lock which coupled it with a catch to the bottom of the bars. To break through would take many minutes of hard work — in full view of the road! He glanced at his watch. Half-past eight, and the pavement busy with passing people, any one of whom might see him at work! It was only by a stroke of luck they hadn't noticed his almost unconscious exit from the safe. It would be well after midnight before he dared move again, so he lay down on the floor behind one of the long show-cases and prepared to sleep, secure in the knowledge he would wake at whatever time he willed.

Not until one in the morning did he consider the streets sufficiently clear for him to begin work. In the past fifteen minutes only one person had walked by, and, judging from the noise he had been making, nothing would have caused that gentleman any surprise.

Before tackling the bars he searched for electric wires which might indicate a burglar alarm; he was reasonably certain there must be one. He was correct, a pair led up from under the floor-boards in the inside of the shop. With insulated wire-cutters he immobilized the alarm.

Carefully listening for any approaching footsteps he worked away at the iron bars, pausing frequently to make certain no alarm had been raised.

At last he finished. Carefully returning the hacksaw to his belt, he stripped off his hood, turned up the collar of his coat, pulled his hat well forward, and swung the iron gate open. As he closed the gate heavy footsteps resounded along the pavement. The next moment a uniformed constable turned into the street from a nearby side road. There was neither time nor opportunity to escape. Blackshirt stood motionless in the faint hope that the constable might not see him, but his optimism was not justified. The policeman saw his black shadow, and suddenly Blackshirt was illuminated in a white circle of light.

"Hello! What's this?" The constable's voice quickened with suspicion, and he raised his whistle to his lips.

"Come here, you fool."

Expecting anything but that reply, the man was taken completely aback.

"What's that?" he demanded in an uncertain voice.

"Will you come off the damned pavement? Come here! Into this doorway." The sharp tones of authority made the policeman move forward. "What's your name?"

"Williams. But who "

"Inspector Maclay. Thanks to your bungling I may have missed Blackshirt."

"How do I know you're an inspector? I wasn't told anyone would be here." The constable was still suspicious.

"Lower your voice — here's my warrant." Blackshirt passed it over — for years he had carried a forged warrant for just such an emergency as this.

"I'm sorry, sir, but no one told me."

"Never mind that. Now you're here you can be of use to me. See that top flat?" He pointed across the road.

119

"Yes, sir."

"If you see the slightest suspicion of a light, blow your whistle. I'm going round the back. We've had word that Blackshirt's making a break there tonight. But whatever you do, don't move from here until I come back. All clear?"

"Yes, sir."

"Stand here, where I am — it's the only place you can clearly see the flat."

The constable moved over as Blackshirt stepped forward, his back to the broken iron bars.

"Remember, Williams, there's a chance of promotion for both of us."

Next moment Blackshirt blithely stepped out on to the pavement, crossed the road and merged into the shadow of the block of buildings opposite, leaving the constable strictly in charge.

*

"More coffee, sir?" asked Roberts.

"Thanks."

The front door bell rang, so Roberts put the coffee-pot down and went to answer it.

A minute later he returned. "Excuse me, sir, but there's a Mr. Jameson would like to see you. I told him you were at breakfast, but he insisted on entering. He made the peculiar statement that it would be better for you if you saw him!"

"Good morning, Verrell." Jameson followed dose on the heels of the valet. Roberts left the room at a sign from Verrell.

"What do you want?" Verrell demanded.

"I'll tell you soon enough." There was a triumphant, sneering expression in Jameson's voice. His mouth twisted into a sly smile.

"Whatever you have to say would you kindly say later. I'm having breakfast. Please leave."

"No, I won't, Mr. Ruddy Blackshirt," said the reporter. Verrell's expression betrayed nothing, though behind this mask his keen brain was trying to meet the sudden disaster that must have overtaken him — else why should the other come out into the open?

"I beg your pardon, what did you call me?"

"You know damn well what I called you — Blackshirt."

"Blackshirt — isn't he the criminal who keeps worrying the Press? Would you mind…"

Jameson leaned forward, his expression harsh. "You can cut out the funny business, Blackshirt, or Verrell, whichever you prefer to be called. I'll tell you just what's happened, so that you can know right where you stand. My paper ordered me to find out who you were — no small order, since the police had failed! But the day after you stole Lancy's invitation to the Carters"*do** I got on your track. He admitted it was queer that someone should know he going and that very few of the guests would know him. He mentioned you, among others, to whom he had talked that evening. He refused even to think of you as Blackshirt. But I don't believe a man's innocent just because he's successful and big."

"Thank you," murmured Verrell drily.

"Don't thank me — you won't feel like it soon! I followed you round. You never knew someone was shadowing you, did you? Nothing happened until the night of that party. You cleared out of your house so suspiciously I became damned certain I was right. You know what happened. I nearly caught you — only I mistook you for the other chap, and didn't bother what was behind me. Blackshirt was there before me and couldn't possibly be Mr. Richard Verrell. But then he spoke and called *me* Blackshirt! You know what happened then and the upshot of it all was that I became the laughing-stock of Fleet Street for my bungling! I got the sack; but when I pleaded for time I was given four days' grace on the condition that I put Blackshirt behind bars. Two days ago I got a letter saying I was sacked anyway. So I'm without a job now — and all through you, you swine! " The reporter's voice was vicious.

"In the meantime I saw Mrs. Sharp and found out you'd been missing at a time when things were happening farther down the road. Said you'd been feeling ill... I bet you were, after the boys had started on you!"

Verrell was dismayed by the tenacity of the reporter, and by the way his own scheme had backfired, leaving him in a tough spot. Had the reporter voiced his suspicions elsewhere? Had he told the police and were they at this moment probing his past? Nevertheless, his voice was casual when he answered: "Am I to believe you are seriously accusing me of being this — er — Blackshirt?"

"Don't you worry — I haven't finished yet."

"I scarcely see any necessity for you to continue. You are being ridiculous."

"I lose my job, fired — and you find it ridiculous! You're clever, I'll grant you that, but this time you've met someone a little cleverer. Who's going to take the word of a poor reporter just thrown out of his job, against a well-known society author? If that's what you're thinking, forget it — and just listen to what I've got to say now." Jameson leaned forward.

"I've met lots of people in my time — queer types some of them. Have you heard of Ropey Man ton? I didn't think you had; he's only a beginner compared with you. I did Ropey a good turn some years ago, and got him out of a nasty jam. Ever since then he's been grateful. Two days ago I saw him and asked him to do a job for me — guess what?

Verrell shrugged his shoulders.

"I asked him to come along and crack a little safe for me! Last night, Blackshirt, while you were burgling the jewellers in the Strand, Ropey and I walked into your flat, and while I held the torch he opened the safe. As soon as he had done that he went, but I returned and looked inside. And there was Mrs. Foley's diamond necklace that you stole at Parkgate House! That was a bad mistake — and it's going to cost you plenty!"

So this was the end to a career — or two careers. Because he had underrated his opponent, he had lost. In less than twenty-four hours headlines would tell the public that at last the incredible Blackshirt had been captured — and that, to add to the excitement, he was none other than Richard Verrell.

"Not so pleasant, is it?" Jameson sneered.

"Why have you told me all this?"

"I got the sack through you. Now you've got to do something for me. I'm going to live in luxury from now on. And it's going to be you who'll do the paying."

"Blackmail?"

"No, not that — such a nasty word! All you are going to do is give me a little pocket-money every so often, when I need it. And just to show there's no ill feeling, I want a couple of hundred right now."

Verrell's thoughts were black. Once in the hands of a blackmailer, only death would release him: his own, or Jameson's. And Verrell knew he could not kill a man in cold blood; criminal he might be, but murderer, never. The alternative: to pay, and pay, and keep on paying. To be bled white by a man who would demand that he rob more frequently to provide yet more hush money. But what else was he to do? One thing was abundantly clear; for the moment he must accede to the reporter's demands. It was that or prison.

Jameson had not misjudged his victim's character when he had dared to walk into the flat alone. He was now equally certain of Verrell's decision.

"And I want it in hard cash, quid notes."

"I haven't that much around."

"A cheque will do."

"Shall I make it out to you?" Verrell spoke in a sharp, controlled voice.

"Not likely. You'll cash it and hand me the notes. No, better still, forward me the money tomorrow morning — or else! Don't bother to see me to the door. I know my way." With a smirk Jameson left.

Chapter Thirteen

Verrell despaired. He looked round his flat, at its comfort and quiet luxury, and winced as he realized it might have to go. The way his banking account would go; the same way the proceeds of innumerable future thefts would go — to the rapacious Jameson, who would milk him dry of everything.

Verrell's thoughts grew blacker until he felt that he must walk, exercise himself, tire his body out. Perhaps an idea would suggest itself. There must be something he could do. At the moment he could think of nothing short of murder.

The front door slammed behind him, and, not caring where he went, he started walking. On and on his legs carried him while he tried to grapple with his problem.

Afterwards, Verrell could not have said where he had been, but realizing he was hungry he looked about him and found he was in Bayswater. Bayswater! Why should that district strike a chord? Janet! Her address was there! And suddenly Verrell had a desire to speak to Janet Dove, to enjoy her company, and forget for a while the problem which beset him.

From a passer-by he learned the whereabouts of the Newgate Hotel, and soon found it. Inside, a bored receptionist manicured her nails and longed for a life of highlights and champagne.

"Pardon me."

She looked up. "Yes, sir, can I help you?"

"I believe Countess Kollinov is staying here?"

"Yes, sir. Room forty-nine. Shall I see if she's in?"

"No thanks' — I'll stroll along and find out."

Verrell knocked at the door of number forty-nine. A very well-known voice, though this time with a slight accent, bade him enter.

"Richard! Well, I'm damned! You really are a clever devil. How in the world did you discover me here? I really thought this would be the last place you'd visit! " Then she noticed his unusually stern expression. "What's wrong? Something worrying you, Richard dear?" She became concerned and showed a side of her character far removed from her usual hard, ruthless self-interest.

"May I sit down?"

"Naturally. But you look as though you'd lost a fortune! " "Janet, have you ever heard of Jameson?"

"No. Should I have done?"

"He was the reporter on the *Daily Star* who wrote those articles about me. And also the chap you noticed following us that day." He paused, deep in thought; then continued. "He knows me as Blackshirt, and intends to make out of it — in other words, blackmail."

"How did he find out?" She didn't waste time in commiseration.

Verrell explained.

"The only proof he could produce in a court of law is the necklace in your safe. The rest wouldn't mean a thing," she said.

"Possibly. But if he mentions his suspicions to the police, though they might not have sufficient proof to arrest me immediately, in time they'd be able to root enough out. Once they get a lead, you've had it, Janet."

"So you daren't challenge the reporter?"

"No."

"In that case there's only one way out of it, kill him!" she said calmly.

Verrell looked up from the floor. She was perfectly serious and it came as something of a shock to him, despite what he knew of her. To her it was a perfectly simple matter. Eliminate Jameson and the trouble ceased.

"I couldn't do that, Janet."

"Why not?"

"I've never killed a man in cold blood. During the war it was different. But I could no more shoot or stab that man than — well, rob a blind beggar."

Janet knew that he had stated the simple truth. It was the inherent decency of Richard Verrell which endeared him to her. He stole for the pleasure of excitement; for the thrill of pitting his wits against others; and for no other reason.

"If I were in your place, I'd take the first way out I could find. I must have wealth and all the things it buys. Good clothes, smooth service, lack of worry and fear. And for that, Richard, I'll fight tooth and nail. And if it becomes necessary to kill, then I'll do it with my own hands — shocked?"

"Not really. I suppose I've always realized it — especially not so many weeks ago." A smile warmed his face, made him look younger. "We all live by a creed — yours is even less citizen-like than mine! Maybe I'm soft, call it what you will."

Janet felt that she wanted to shake him — loosen some of his ideas!

"Richard, we've got to do something, you can't carry on like this. Let's go out today. Take me to a show or cinema; it'll clear your mind and mine; and then, maybe, we'll think of something."

"I'd love it, but my company won't be exactly cheerful."

"Nonsense! Just give me five minutes and I'll be ready."

In rather more than the five minutes Janet was ready to leave, a charming figure, exquisitely dressed. Her beautiful, vivacious features affected even Blackshirt's mood.

"You're looking wonderful."

"Thank you, sir." She curtsied ironically, and then glanced downwards so that her eyes might not reveal her thoughts. She claimed that luxury and wealth were her ideals in life; that she wanted nothing more. She was lying — and she knew it.

*

"Richard, you might listen! I've been speaking to you for five minutes and you haven't heard a word."

"I'm sorry, Janet," he apologized.

She leaned over and touched his hand for an instant. "Suppose you had proof that this Jameson was Blackshirt. Absolutely irrevocable proof — wouldn't that put you in a position where you could tell him where to go?"

"It would; but I might have a little trouble in securing such proof!"

"If you had a photo of him in Blackshirt clothes actually burgling a safe, I'm certain it would put the fear of God into him. He sounds the type of bully who's very brave until something goes wrong. Hold that threat over him and he'd crumple up like a rotten melon."

"No, Janet. He'd say he'd been forced into posing for the picture. When the police started searching our respective pasts they'd soon find out that he couldn't be Blackshirt, and then they'd want to know how, when, and why I'd got hold of the photo."

"He'd never dare contact them."

"Yes, he would.2

"Not if there was something else besides. If you planted a ring or something in his flat."

"I thought of all that and it's just not worth while."

"But, Richard…" Janet argued and argued, eliminating each of Verrell's objections one by one. Where he was inclined to be pessimistic — she was optimistic. Where he flatly denied a possibility — she as flatly affirmed its probability. Finally he agreed to try out her suggestion.

Janet was grateful. It had been a long battle and one that she could not have won, had Blackshirt's mind been more alert — since he would have realized the weakness of the whole scheme.

Silently she grappled with the problem. The problem of what would actually happen in two nights' time — in accordance with her principles, not his!

*

Jameson cursed his bad luck as he undressed prior to a large night-cap and bed. He had lost over a hundred pounds at the game of poker. Angered by this he had accused Herb of cheating. Blows were avoided only when the other three intervened between the two slightly drunk men. Taken all in all it had been a foul evening and had given him a foul head. One thing was certain. The next morning he'd milk Verrell for another five hundred. There was not the slightest reason why the cracksman shouldn't pay him well for keeping quiet. Damn him! with his gentlemanly ways, his fine speech and manners — all a ruddy farce, since he was a crook. When Jameson thought of the scorn that had been so apparent in the other's eyes he swore in anger.

Right now he decided he might phone Sylvia to see...

"If I were you, Jameson, I'd put that down."

Startled, the reporter swung round. Ten feet away were two figures in black, each holding a revolver. The shock sobered his brain.

"What — Blackshirt"

"Put that receiver down."

He did as he was ordered. For a wild moment he thought it might be a nightmare; but the figures remained, ominously like hooded executioners in appearance. He grew intensely afraid.

"Listen, Blackshirt. I was only joking when I said I wanted so much money. Honestly, I never intended to ask you for any more. You must believe me. I would have forgotten everything I ever learned about you."

There was no reply.

"Say something. I can't stand it, I..." He tailed off as the second figure moved forward in grim silence and threw down a brown paper package.

"Inside," said Blackshirt, "you'll find a black shirt, a pair of black trousers, gloves and a mask. Carry this parcel with you. Right now get dressed — you're coming with us."

"Where to? What are you going to do?"

"You'll find out soon enough. Hurry up and get some clothes on." He pointed with the automatic to the door. In ten minutes Jameson was fully dressed in large overcoat and hat that, on being ordered, he pulled down over his eyes. Under the clothing he was shivering.

"Pick that parcel up and follow me. If you make the slightest sound we'll shoot."

"All right, start moving." Janet spoke for the first time.

At the sound of a woman's voice, Jameson started. Blackshirt with a woman! Who could she be, this accomplice? And if there were a woman present, surely they were not going to do him any harm. For the first time he began to hope, and as he did so, to scheme. No woman would be as grim, callous as Blackshirt — surely, she would listen to him if he could get the chance to speak to her. That was it. He must get her on her own. It was with some degree of self-possession that he followed Blackshirt down to the front door. Just before leaving the darkened flat the other two had taken off their hoods.

Directly outside the door was a car of ordinary make, no different from thousands of others. Blackshirt opened the rear door and first Jameson then Janet climbed in to the back, while Blackshirt took the driver's seat and started the engine.

For over an hour the car drove on, through part of London that Jameson was familiar with and then into the countryside, where, beyond knowing that they were moving in a southerly direction, he was lost. Meanwhile, by quick glances, whenever the car was illuminated by street lights or by another car's headlamps, the reporter realized that the woman by his side must be young; and, even though half her features were covered by the upturned lapels of her coat and her hat, he decided that she was one of the most attractive women he had seen. He found himself moving to try and see her more clearly. She withdrew her right hand and pointed a gun steadily at him. He moved back into his own corner.

The car turned off to the right of the main road, and for two miles proceeded down a country lane. Then another turn to the right, and four hundred yards down a rutted track. It came to a halt in front of a ramshackle barn.

Blackshirt stopped the car, got out, opened the back door, and waited while the two descended.

"Follow me and bring that parcel with you."

"Why should I? Listen, Blackshirt, you're going to"

"I said follow me." His voice was grim.

If Jameson were to obtain mercy, it was not from the man.

"I'm staying here for half a minute," said Janet.

Blackshirt was surprised, but he prodded Jameson in the back with his revolver and indicated a path that led through a copse of trees.

Jameson understood. He was to be killed by Blackshirt. The woman was staying behind since she could not face the actual murder. He started to plead for mercy. The only reply was another wave in the direction of the path and the muttered caution:

"Shut up. Don't bother to call out — there's nothing within miles."

The reporter stumbled along the narrow path and then into a small field, where Blackshirt called a halt to wait for Janet.

She took some time to join them and her breathing was hurried. But, disregarding Blackshirt's query, she made a suggestion.

"You go on ahead, I'll wait here with him. Come back as soon as you've found it's all clear."

Blackshirt merged into the shadows and disappeared.

In an instant Jameson swung round. "Tell me — what are you going to do?"

"Do you really want to know?"

"Yes," he mumbled.

"Kill you. Dress you up in Blackshirt's clothes, those you brought along, and leave your body in the empty house — to be found at some future date." She spoke quite calmly.

Jameson shivered. Before the night was out he would be dead. He grew desperately afraid. "You — you can't. *You* can't stand by and watch him kill me in cold blood?"

"I won't be there."

"For God's sake what have I done- — to be shot like a dog? I — I only asked for a loan, honest. I swear that was all."

"Your 'loan' smelt more like blackmail."

"It wasn't; I swear it by anything you want. I like him, I like him a lot. I wouldn't blackmail him. Maybe I did find out he was Blackshirt, but I wouldn't tell another living soul. I wouldn't have done — never I —"

Janet seemed to be taking no notice of his impassioned plea.

"I don't mean Blackshirt harm. But I can't explain in his present mood, he wouldn't listen. But you know I don't. You must know."

"I"

"Help me — help me, otherwise I'll be dead before morning — and he'll be *a* — a murderer. You can't just stand by." "What do you want me to do?" she asked in a worried voice.

Jameson's hopes leapt. The woman was falling for his line! If only Blackshirt would keep away for another few minutes he might get free. Then, tomorrow, Blackshirt would have cause to remember him.

"If you'll give me a chance. A break to get away — just turn your back for a second. I'll repay your kindness a thousand fold, I promise. He's mad to want to kill me."

For a moment she did not reply, then, "What will you do?"

"Get away in the car."

"Blackshirt's got a fast sports car to return in."

"That doesn't matter. I'll drive so damn quickly he'll never catch me. Once I'm near town he'd never dare to shoot. Tomorrow morning I'll explain everything, I promise."

"Well, I "

"Please."

"You're certain you want to drive away in the car we came in?"

"Of course I'm certain. It's life or death. Life or death, can't you understand?" he snapped, forgetting for the moment his role.

"All right. I tried to stop his killing you. Will you promise solemnly that you'll hold nothing against him? I'd never forgive myself if any trouble came through letting you loose."

"I swear by all that I hold sacred that nothing whatsoever will come of it."

Janet lowered her weapon. "I feel sorry for you. Now go; and you'd better hurry, I can hear him returning." Jameson raced for the car and started it, thanking his lucky stars that the key had been left in. Then, with gears grinding, he raced off at top speed — his only thought to get away.

Janet gazed sombrely at the retreating car, then sighed. He had gone of his own free will. So she could not really accuse herself — the nuts of the front wheels of any car might be loose. With a shrug she dismissed the matter. When one was fighting for the safety of someone whom one lov — liked, then anything went.

Panting, Verrell retraced his steps.

"Did I hear a car?"

"Yes."

"Not ours? Where's Jameson?"

"Escaped. Ran off just like that! I couldn't bring myself to shoot him there and then. I'm sorry, Blackshirt, I've failed — the whole scheme's failed…" She could no longer hold back her tears. Blackshirt placed a comforting arm around her.

"It doesn't matter, Janet. I knew it wouldn't work, but you were so insistent. For goodness' sake don't worry, it'll all work out, one way or the other." He paused. "The only question now is — how do we get home?"

Smiling up at him through her tears, Janet said, "I noticed another car parked a mile or so back along the road. If it's still there we'll be O.K."

Arm in arm they walked up the track and along the lane. As Janet had prophesied, a large sports car was parked just off the road, with the key in the dashboard.

Ten minutes later, Verrell had to stop. An ambulance and a police car surrounded some wreckage to the side of the road. A policeman came up to the car. "If you pull right over, providing your offside wheel comes up against the bank, you'll be able to get by, sir."

"Thanks. Filthy accident."

"Very, sir. Must have been travelling too speedily for such a small car; both front wheels came off, found them back of the hedge, crashed into that telegraph pole. Never had a chance, poor chap. Newspaper reporter, according to some papers we found."

A wild hope flashed through Verrell's mind.

"What was his name? Any of the well-known ones? Care for a cigarette?"

"Thank you, sir, not while I'm on duty. Jameson was the name — can't say I've heard of him before. Have you?"

"I don't think so, no. Well, good night."

"Good night, sir. Keep hard up against the bank."

On the way into London, Verrell hummed a tune, more atrociously out of key than usual. He felt no hypocritical regret at the reporter's death. He was a thoroughly dis-likable type, and he had threatened Verrell's future.

Janet looked up at him, and noticed the smile. Because his eyes were dancing with relief and humour she felt compensated. He would never know the truth, *must* never know the truth- — for if he did, he might never see her again. Her Blackshirt had principles, and sometimes she did not know whether they were an asset, or a drawback.

Inside the hotel, she suggested they should go up to her room and have a drink.

"Bit late, isn't it, Janet?"

"Don't be silly, Richard. We've got something to celebrate."

Together they walked up to her room. She unlocked her door, entered and switched on the light.

"Good evening," greeted the Jackdaw.

Chapter Fourteen

He stood up as they entered.

"What — what are you doing here?" asked Janet, in a worried voice.

"Came to see how you were getting on," he replied cheerfully. "After all, we never settled up with regards to our little partnership — or had the fact escaped your memory?" Janet ignored him and taking off her coat threw it on to the back of a chair. For the first time Peebles noticed that both she and Verrell were wearing black shirts.

"Well I'm damned! Blackshirt giving you a few lessons?

Never knew you looked so smart in trousers, Janet. Not many women can wear them without looking utter fools." He smiled sardonically. Janet shrugged her shoulders angrily.

"Blackshirt, what was the name of those people in Newark Road, the ones that owned the house?"

"Longton," he replied easily, a smile lurking in his eyes.

"Janet," said Peebles in ominous tones, "what the devil did you choose that place for — and who were those interfering puppies?"

Janet looked startled. "What on earth are you talking about?"

"You know damned well what I'm talking about."

"It's quite possible she doesn't," interrupted Blackshirt easily, "since I never mentioned it to her."

"Never mentioned it," he repeated stupidly. "But it was her idea."

"As a matter of fact it was my idea entirely, but it didn't work out. Sorry about those rugger players, but I wasn't expecting them either. Still, you'll be glad to know that everything worked out all right in the end."

"I — I..." He couldn't speak for rage. Nor was he appeased when a delighted Janet requested the details, and laughed whole-heartedly at the conclusion.

"All's well that ends well," said Janet soothingly, feeling that Peebles would take violent action if they pursued the subject any farther. "How about a drink? What's yours? I can offer sherry, or gin and something."

Peebles muttered something which the other two didn't catch; from the expression on his face it was just as well. Then in a sullen voice he asked for a gin and tonic. The conversation was quiet until Peebles had finished his drink. Then he stood up and lounged across to the door leading outside. Blackshirt glanced at Janet and saw her face stiffen.

"If you remember, Blackshirt, we had a small arrangement between us — that whoever found Janet should tell the other. I'm still waiting." His voice had hardened.

"As a matter of fact I only met Janet this evening," he replied easily.

The Jackdaw regarded him in silence for a moment.

Janet made as if to move from the arm-chair, but at a savage gesture from him she relaxed.

"I read in the papers that someone had stolen a valuable pair of pearl ear-rings from a jewellery shop in the Strand; it didn't take long to put two and two together. I reckoned it was Blackshirt who had got them, and that they were part of the Darthweight collection. That meant that you had a lead on Janet. There's only one thing Harry's any good at, and that's shadowing. He followed you for a whole morning — not like you, Blackshirt, to be caught napping — and finally to this hotel. Now there's only one more thing — where are the pearls?"

"1 haven't got them," said Janet.

"Where have you left them?"

"That's none of your business," she flashed.

"We've been through most of your baggage and there's no deposit slip — and no pearls."

"You filthy brute," snapped Janet. "Have you been pawing through my luggage?"

"Not so much I as Harry and Jim. Unless you've got them on you, you've stowed them either in here or the bathroom or bedroom. It'll save a lot of trouble if you'll say where."

"You can go and whistle for them."

"I'm not worried by scruples like Blackshirt," he sneered. "I'll strip every piece of clothing off you if necessary. And if that doesn't work I'll leave you to Jim and Harry. Perhaps you didn't know how mad they are. You can yell as much as you like, but I doubt if anyone will hear you — Jim's responsible for that. As for Harry — he's very clever at making people talk! "

Janet's face was white.

"Peebles, you " Blackshirt spoke hurriedly.

"Can't do it?" he broke in. "Don't be a sap, Blackshirt. Janet's got those pearls and I mean to have them. And for your own good keep quiet. The boys won't hurt her more than necessary."

Blackshirt tensed himself. Anything rather than to have to stand by whilst they tortured Janet. Peebles noticed the movement.

"Harry. Jim." he called out.

The two men rushed in from the bedroom.

"If Blackshirt moves an inch — shoot. Got it?"

"Be a ruddy pleasure," muttered Harry grimly.

Slowly Blackshirt relaxed. He could do absolutely nothing for the moment. The three men were roughly in a semicircle. The moment he rose from the arm-chair they would shoot and leave him incapable of helping Janet. Alive he might yet turn the tables. Dead or crippled, he would be useless. Janet gave him a brave smile and shook her head. As she looked away she bit her lip.

"For the last time, Janet, where are the pearls?"

"I tell you I haven't got them."

"Don't be a little fool. I'm not playing. Either you hand them over or I'll make you wish you had. If Blackshirt knows anything he'd better speak — because he'll be watching you kick!"

Blackshirt leapt up from the chair, his self-control gone. But before he had taken a step forward Jim brought a life-preserver down on his head, and he fell to the floor unconscious. Janet, ignoring the others, bent down to help him.

"He's all right," growled thg Jaekdaw. "Jim knows what he's doing. Be round in a couple of minutes. Tie his hands up," he ordered.

When Blackshirt recovered consciousness only Peebles and Janet were in the room. As he went to rub his aching head, he discovered his hands were bound.

"You utter swine," he said, "if you lay one hand on Janet I'll..." He groaned as the pain became worse.

"Don't talk," said Janet, her voice taut. "It'll only amuse him."

At that moment the silence was shattered by the violent ringing of alarm bells.

Peebles cursed. "What the devil's all the fuss about?" Just then all three noticed a thin tendril of smoke curling under the door, and from outside came a panic-stricken shout of "*fire!*".

"Hell! The sooner we get out of here the better," there was alarm in his voice, and for a moment he rushed backwards and forwards across the room.

Janet's lips curled in disdain at the swift transition from bullying bravado to panic-stricken fright. Quickly she released Blackshirt's hands.

"Where's the fire-escape?" panted the Jackdaw.

"Haven't a clue," she replied scornfully, half-way to the bedroom.

"Don't just stand there! Which is the way out?" Without waiting for an answer Peebles rushed to the door, opened it, and the next second disappeared down the corridor.

"Come on, Janet, the sooner we're outside the better." Blackshirt spoke urgently — the smoke was becoming thicker. Rapidly he drew the white scarf round his neck to hide the black shirt. Janet did not reply, but shut the bedroom door, and, if he had heard aright, locked it. He smiled. Even in their present predicament she trusted no one.

When Janet returned, she had changed into a blouse and skirt, and was carrying two small leather bags.

"Here, give them to me," he said.

"I'll hang on to this one."

Together they made their way downstairs as quickly as the dense smoke and scurrying people would allow.

Guests and staff were milling around outside the main entrance, but were quickly ushered to one side as the two fire-engines pulled up. Hoses were connected, and firemen, wearing smoke helmets, entered the building.

In a few minutes they were back with their report — the smoke had been caused by a mixture of chemicals — there were no flames, no fire.

"Whoever caused that false alarm," remarked Verrell, later, "certainly did us a good turn! Peebles revealed himself as uncommonly vicious."

Janet shuddered. "We might as well return and finish our drink." She turned abruptly. "Richard, have you got my bag?"

"Not the one yop insisted on carrying."

"But I put it down beside me, when the fire-engine turned up." Her voice rose. "Where on earth can it have got to, Richard?"

An idea flashed into Verrell's mind. A crazy idea, maybe, but...

"Tanet, what did you have in the bag?"

"Clothes."

"And the pearls?"

"Well, I..." she gulped. "Yes."

Verrell laughed. Loud, joyous laughter that brought tears to his eyes.
"RichardI What's so funny?"

"Don't you see, Janet — the fire — Peebles arranged it — Jim and Harry
went out — he knew that if you had them you'd save them before anything
else…"

Verrell's laughter was tinged with admiration for the absent Peebles.

*

On his way home Verrell continued to grin. For a while Janet had
informed him, and anyone else who cared to listen, precisely what she
thought of Peebles. Then, turning on him because he could do nothing but
laugh, she had, at last, joined him in his amusement.

Before he left her he had promised to meet her the following morning
and discuss a fresh plan of campaign to recover the pearls. Though even
Janet had to admit that she had no idea where to begin.

Verrell switched on the light in his flat. He changed into pyjamas and a
dressing-gown, and returned to the sitting-room where he lit a cigarette.
From the depths of his armchair he gazed affectionately round the room.
He sincerely hoped that never again would he come so close to losing
everything. His mind wandered in easy stages to the problem of his safe. A
stronger one was essential — frequently incriminating evidence would be
in it for months, maybe a particular piece of jewellery which he liked to
gloat over, enjoying the sheer pleasure of something well-nigh perfect. If
he bought a really modern safe, even though it would have to be small, it
must be burglar proof and if he couldn't give a studied opinion on that
point, who could? It must fit in the same place, behind a painting, since
otherwise it would introduce a jarring note into the room which he had
furnished with such taste.

Gazing at the painting, Verrell became puzzled. Something looked odd.
A small square of white was stuck in the lower corner. As he neared it he
could read the typewritten words.

"Thanks — The Jackdaw," was all it said.

There was even less inside the safe — it had been swept clear!

"Well I'm damned!" murmured Blackshirt.

*

Verrell had arranged a luncheon date with Janet for twelve-thirty.
Knowing her habits as he did, he was not surprised when Roberts
announced her at ten.

"What have you done about it?"

"Nothing yet, Janet, I've only just had my breakfast."

"At a time like this all you can do is eat breakfast! " she said in a sharp voice.

"Instead of grumbling, have some coffee. I'll tell Roberts to make some more."

"No thanks. And for goodness sake shake yourself up. I've been up since the crack of dawn trying to get a line on Peebles."

"And you found nothing?"

"No," she admitted in a small voice.

"I could have told you that last night, Janet. If I'd thought there was any chance of Peebles returning home I'd have suggested our going straight there. But I'd have given you any odds you liked that he had moved."

"You'd have won! " She sounded, and looked, tired.

"Change your mind and have some coffee, it'll buck you up."

"All right. I'm sorry, Richard, but I haven't had a wink of sleep. Those pearls meant so much to me and now I don't know what to do. I might even have to take a job."

Verrell forbore to laugh at the thought of Janet working in an office. "Surely things can't be so bad as that?"

"Nearly. After I've paid the hotel bill, I'll have less than ten pounds left. I was banking on the ear-rings for ready money — and you didn't give me a chance." Janet applied a scrap of lace to the corner of each eye, at the same time covertly watching him. If she knew her Verrell the offer should be immediate. But, to her consternation, it wasn't. "Those ear-rings — Janet, I — as a matter of fact Peebles stole them last night before I returned!" he admitted with obvious reluctance.

Janet gurgled. It certainly was not the outcome she had hoped for, but still…

"What do we do now? It seems so absolutely hopeless — he's probably already got rid of them. I know he had a market lined up."

"I suppose you don't know who?"

"No. He wouldn't tell me."

"I can't think why."

Janet had to smile. "But you must be able to do something. With all the contacts you have, there's somebody who will know."

"I doubt it, Janet. If the Jackdaw had his market there's no reason to suspect anyone else will be connected with the deal. He won't have to work through a fence."

"You're really helpful!" Her mouth drooped. Then in a more cheerful voice she asked, "What about the man we were going to deal with? He must have had someone in view or he would never have offered to buy jewels so well known. Why, the odds are it's the same person! Richard, you must go and ask him right away, now! "

"My dear Janet, remember the saying about patience." "Patience fiddlesticks!"

"In the first case the odds against the two unknowns being the same are high. "

"No they aren't."

"Secondly, I couldn't visit Otto before tonight. He's nocturnal in his habits!"

"In that case you'll go tonight."

"I really can't see."

"Just for me."

Verrell, looking into Janet's eyes, decided that he would go. In fact, if Janet looked at him like that again and asked him to steal the Crown Jewels, he would have a try!

*

"Have a drink, my friend?"

"No thanks, Otto."

"Of course. Tell me, Blackshirt, what have you for me this time? What are you going to try and sell me at four times the proper value? Always I think, when you turn up, I see the most wonderful of gems. I admire your taste, my dear Blackshirt, only less than your amazing luck."

"I haven't anything for you this time. I want something." "Such as?" Speyer's amiability underwent a subtle change. His mouth tightened and his hand moved towards a drawer.

"Information."

Speyer relaxed.

"Yes?"

"I want to know what you've heard within the past two days regarding the Darthweight pearls."

"The pearls you were going to sell to me?"

"Yes."

"And now you aren't?"

"You know I'm not! "

"What have I heard about them, *hein*? What would you like me to say?"

"Listen, Speyer, you like living as much as I do — you like your freedom as much as I." Blackshirt's eyes had hardened, his voice was crisp. "I want to know, and quickly."

"Threats, my dear Blackshirt?" But Speyer's voice was not so certain. He had always been at a disadvantage with this unknown person.

"Yes — if you like to put it that way."

"You don't need to threaten, Blackshirt. We're old friends. I'm pleased to tell you what I know. I've heard of them in the last few hours. They have been sold for sixty thousand pounds."

"Sixty! Is that what you were offered?"

Speyer almost blushed, and hastily covered up the *faux pas* with a nervous cough.

"To whom were they sold?"

"I don't know."

Blackshirt, momentarily elated at the prospect of tracing the elusive pearls, was disappointed. After all, it *had* been a forlorn chance.

Speyer chuckled softly.

"But I could guess, Blackshirt, I could guess."

"For Pete's sake, then, hurry up and do so."

"It's my guess," he leaned forward, "that they went to Edward Vernon."

The information brought no gladness to Blackshirt's heart. He knew Vernon was supposed to own nearly a million pounds' worth of jewellery — but he had also heard about Rando Castle, where the collection was housed.

After the Bank of England, it was possibly the most carefully guarded place in England.

Otto chuckled. "If you're thinking of the possibility, I don't think I should! At least two people have tried — one's doing seven years, and the other five. Even Blackshirt hasn't a chance! "

"Maybe?"

"My friend, so impossible is it that I would offer you a thousand to one that you'd never succeed."

"Taken; one pound to a thousand, Otto — and first refusal of the jewellery." There was a lilt in his voice. A carefree expression that said, be damned to the facts. "You are not serious?"

"Here's my pound."

"Blackshirt, my friend, if you try you will end up in prison. And then —
where would I get my exquisite jewellery from?"

But Blackshirt had already left — and on the table rested a pound note!

Chapter Fifteen

Janet was waiting for Blackshirt in his flat.

"Well, Richard?"

"Well, what?"

"Don't be ridiculous. Have you discovered who's got them?"

"Yes."

"You have I" She clapped her hands. "How soon can we set about reclaiming our possessions — it's funny, but I feel it's an obligation to get them back."

"Whose obligation — yours or mine?"

"Ours, of course I Will you please say where they are?"

"In Rando Castle. That is, so far as is known. Otto seemed to think that was by far the most likely place."

Janet's eyes dulled. "Rando Castle. Oh! Blackshirt; they might as well be at the bottom of the sea. Isn't it just like Peebles to sell them to him! Good-bye my holiday in Spain."

"Yes, I'm afraid it's utterly impossible — and yet I've just had a bet on the result. Otto gave me a thousand to one that I wouldn't succeed."

"And you took the bet?"

"Yes."

"Richard, you're incorrigible. Surely you know by now when a thing's impossible?"

"Yes."

"Well, why throw your money away?"

"I seldom do."

"Do you mean you are actually going to try?"

"Yes, of course."

Tanet drew in a deep, satisfied breath. "When do we start?"

"I start as soon as possible."

"We you mean."

"Janet, you're not going to have anything to do with it."

The argument was long.

*

142

Rando Castle lay on a rise overlooking the village of Duckstaff. The castle had been built in the twelfth century, since when ill-assorted additions had been made at intervals.

In the centre was the keep. A square stone edifice with large kitchen and domestic quarters half sunk beneath the ground, and three floors above. Encircling the keep was a fortified castellated wall with archer's slits set at intervals. A dry moat surrounded this, access to the castle being possible by way of a tunnelled passage beneath the outer wall, closed at the outer end by wooden gates, and at the inner end by a portcullis which was sometimes lowered for effect.

Over the centuries, the castle, remaining in the same branch of one family, had slowly decayed with the fortunes of the family until it was in a fair way to becoming a ruin.

The owners had been forced to sell, and Edward Vernon had bought Rando Castle. Money had been poured into restoring and modernizing it. The keep was transformed into a luxurious residence. The first floor was retained for receptions, and the huge rooms left unpartitioned. The second floor was divided into a number of relatively small and comfortable living-rooms and guest bedrooms. Half the third floor was given over to the Vernons' private suite, the other half to guest rooms larger than those on the floor below. On the battlements the new owner had added two rooms reached by a circular staircase. The first was his private library, and it led into the second room, to which there was no other means of access. This was the room which housed his safe — and where he spent much of his time.

No servants lived in the keep. Their quarters were against the outer wall, in buildings originally erected in the seventeenth century.

In the process of modernization nothing had been spared in an effort to suggest authenticity. The portcullis, ten feet from the moat, had been repaired, made good with genuine old timber where necessary, and kept hoisted so that only its long, pointed base projected.

Edward Vernon was a curious mixture. He had started as an office boy in a shipping firm owned by his uncle, on the understanding that he should pass through each side of the business before taking over. His uncle had died some five years later, leaving Edward the owner of two tramp ships whose days were strictly numbered and hardly insurable. Profits were absent. The firm's survival was in the balance when the Spanish Civil War broke out. Gun-running, contraband cargoes, and illegal transportation of refugees proved so remunerative that, despite the loss of two vessels captured, he owned at the conclusion of that war twenty-four vessels, mostly new.

A year of cut-throat, price-slashing competition and he had a good trade to the South Americas. By the end of the Second Great War, Vernon's fleet was more than thirty vessels, plus twelve sunk, which would be reimbursed by the Government. A few years of peaceful business, during which time he ruined two rivals, and Edward Vernon found himself one of the, if not the, richest man in England. It was then he set about becoming a gentleman.

He was a dismal failure. Despite his immense wealth, and a certain natural charm, he had a coarseness he could not conceal. He was vulgar in his boast of what he owned, vulgar in his ways of life, and vulgar in his manners. He might even have overcome this had he not been married. His wife was unanimously declared to be the end.

When Vernon found that he was unable to make his way into society, he withdrew with bitter hate, and started to collect jewellery. This became a mania to such an extent that he spent hour after hour gloating over his possessions. Everything was grist to his mill. He bought, irrespective of price or legality.

As the mania increased, so did his fear of theft. The domestic staff was reduced to a minimum, that he might have less chance to fear treachery. At the same time he installed armed guards, whose sole job was to patrol the grounds and buildings. Whenever he opened his safe two men guarded the entrance to the library. To the outside world it all provided a huge joke and cartoonists relied on him to provide material when all else failed. But as the value of his collection neared seven figures, perhaps the joke was on the other foot.

*

"One gin and tonic, one gin and French, please."

"Yes, sir."

Janet and Verrell were the only people present, apart from the landlord, and as soon as the drinks had been served, Verrell found no difficulty in engaging him in conversation. From items of general interest, the discussion was adroitly steered round to Rando Castle and its owner. The landlord gave sharp vent to his feelings.

" 'Tain't as though I were prejudiced, sir. You ask anyone round these parts, and they'll tell you the same. He don't take a hap'orth of interest in any one of us. When old Lord Hansbury had the castle, in ruins it might be, but the old 'uns declare he were the finest man to work for in the land. He looked after us all, knew our first names — and wasn't above stoppin' to have a chat when he felt like it. But this here man don't know one of us from t'other — ain't interested. He don't look after his farms, or the people what has to live in them. Near failin' down some of them be. And he ain't no gentleman, neither, and none of the gentlefolk hereabouts call on him. He treats his staff terrible. Always leaving they are. All he can do is sit day after day staring at them jewels what don't do no good to man nor beast."

He paused. Verrell called for another round of drinks. The landlord poured them out, including a pint of bitter for himself. He raised the glass, and lowered it, empty. Wiping his mouth with the back of his hand he continued talking.

"No, I ain't got many good words for 'im, and I ain't heard anyone else what has. The way he lives you'd think he was a jaggering king, begging the lady's pardon. Guards here, guards there. Even the tradespeople can't enter unless they're recognized. Herbert, runs the baker's van, was ill one day, so Fred ups and offers to do it for him. Arrives at the gate, and darn me if they didn't hold him up 'til they found out he were real 1 "

Another customer walked into the bar, to be closely followed by three more, and soon talk became general. After a further fifteen minutes Janet and Verrell rose and, to a chorus of "good nights" from the friendly inmates, left.

"Now what, Richard?"

"I suggest we go and have a looksee. After all, who knows, we might find a hidden passage that leads straight up inside the safe! "

But, despite his cheerful words, Janet realized that for the moment he was stumped.

Their visit did nothing to reverse his opinion. The moat and wall formed an insurmountable obstacle, and the landlord had said that a fly couldn't get through the one gateway either by day or by night.

"That's that," said Blackshirt blankly. Even Janet had to agree. In glum silence they started to retrace their steps. They had not gone a hundred yards when a car drove slowly past them, then stopped.

"Want a lift?" A small, precise-looking man stuck his head out of the rear window.

Verrell remembered that Janet and he had deliberately worn old and slightly shabby mackintoshes, which gave them the appearance of an ill-paid clerk and his wife. He was on the point of refusing when the other continued, "Mr. Vernon back there don't allow anyone to travel in this car but his own staff — since we, that's the wife and I, are leaving in a week's time, I don't see why we shouldn't show him where to put his orders! "

Verrell answered. "We'd love to go to the village, wouldn't we, Gert? Never driven in one of these big cars before."

Janet giggled.

Once in, Verrell offered sympathy. "Sorry to hear you're leaving. You don't look the kind of couple that would give anyone offence."

"We're not," he answered sharply, "but we've been used to the best houses 1 Only last week my wife said she couldn't lower herself much longer — and when he wanted a meal served at three in the morning that did it."

"So I should think! That's no way to treat a cook."

"I'm butler, and my wife housekeeper. Butler and housekeeper and the whole staff is fewer than ten!"

"Ten in a house that big?" Janet said in a surprised tone of voice.

"That's right — and then, I'm the only man apart from all those guards. Said outright he didn't trust no men, on account of them jewels."

"Don't seem right to me."

"No more it would to any respectable butler! It's the first — and last — house that I've ever had to carry coal! But I couldn't see the poor maids staggering up them steps with great buckets full.

There were further words of commiseration.

"Very proper. What are you going to do now?"

"Go back to the agency; see they get us a decent job this time. No ruddy workhouse for me. That so, Emma?"

"Yes, Herbert, it is. I'll not take a job like that again! " The chauffeur brought the car to a halt at the station, where Verrell and Janet thanked the other two for their kindness. They then left the station and returned to their own car, parked in a side street.

On the drive home, Janet was pessimistic, while Verrell remained non-committal. At last Janet, annoyed by his inattention, sharply asked him if he'd prefer her to walk home.

"I'm sorry, Janet, I was thinking."

"What about? I've been talking to you for hours and you haven't heard a word of what I said!"

"Rando Castle, of course."

"Pleasant subject for thought, isn't it? You can't get in, you can't get out; and if you could you'd just become a free meal for the dogs. I could murder that wretched Peebles!"

"Things wouldn't be quite so difficult if one could wander through the house, would they?" His voice was thoughtful.

"Now what's on your mind? Knock at the front door, and say you're his school pal from the lower fourth; or the back door, and say you're the new butler?"

"That's right," replied Verrell.

*

The firm of Masons claimed to be the largest employment agency for domestic workers. It catered, in general, for the larger establishments who required butlers, housekeepers, chefs and thoroughly trained staffs. They charged a heavy premium, which was justified since they usually offered excellent jobs.

Their premises were situated just off Oxford Street. Verrell entered the waiting-room and sat down. The walls were covered with newspaper cuttings from 'jobs vacant' columns; and on the tables were a scattered assortment of journals and trade papers. A small desk, heaped with index cards, indicated a secretary.

Shortly afterwards a harassed, white-faced woman appeared through a door marked 'Private', made for the desk, but seeing someone waiting asked his business.

"Have you an appointment?"

"No, I'm afraid not."

"I don't know if he'll be able to see you — still it's not a busy day. What's your name, please."

"Martin."

"Your position?"

"Butler."

"Have you brought your references with you?"

"Yes."

He produced a bulky packet of papers. These had cost him a visit to Mr. 'Bluey' Wexley, and also several bank notes. They were guaranteed authentic.

"You keep them. I'll see if Mr. Jeans is busy."

After twenty minutes, during which time 'Martin' started to light a cigarette and was severely rebuked for doing so, he was shown into the office.

A small man, seated before a desk, looked up. Having made certain that Martin had not applied to his agency before, he added five per cent to his fee. He looked through the references, asked several questions, and handed them back. He then asked what kind of position was required.

"Butler."

"Yes, quite; but I want to know in what part of the country, what type of household, and at what salary."

"I don't mind what kind of house, but large ones for preference. Always adds a kind of dignity, I reckon."

The other nodded his head in agreement.

"Salary the same as my last employment; if possible not too far from London. I have a cousin I like visiting occasionally."

"Um! Nothing near London to suit you, I'm afraid. There's only one job going, and that's for a married couple, wife to act as housekeeper. Very nice place — there's little company and everyone says it can be made quite cosy — only trouble is, the old boy's a collector and likes food served up at odd times of the day and night. You're not interested, I suppose?"

Verrell tried to conceal his amusement. "My wife was housekeeper with two big families before I married her."

Within ten minutes, Mr. and Mrs. Martin were provisionally engaged as butler and housekeeper to Edward Vernon. Their interview would be in two days' time.

Janet was waiting in the Savoy Grill when Verrell, who had rushed back and changed, entered. She smiled fondly at him as he walked over and sat down.

"Any luck?" she asked with eagerness.

"I am now butler to Edward Vernon. Yes, sir; no, sir!"

Janet laughed softly, as she pictured Blackshirt. "I don't expect you'll be much use, probably spill the soup down his front."

"Thank you! But you'll be able to instruct me on points like that."

"I?" she asked, amazed.

"Yes, you."

"But why me?"

"I forgot to mention — you're the housekeeper, my wife," added Verrell maliciously.

Edward Vernon was in a temper — nothing extraordinary. He had been unable to buy a set of emerald rings which had just been sold privately. Hearing of the impending transaction, he had stepped in and offered more than the price already agreed upon. To his annoyance, and amazement, this offer had been firmly rejected.

His wife was annoyed because she had not been invited to an annual ball held nearby; she never was. And before she went out she vented some of her ill-humour on her husband. It was therefore in a surly tone that he interviewed the prospective butler and housekeeper.

"Your name Martin?"

"Yes, sir."

He snorted; he did not like young men, they so often proved impudent and insolent. Though, he had to admit, this particular one looked capable, was neatly dressed, and deferential.

Then he turned his eyes to the wife — and started. Previous housekeepers had been dowdy and uninteresting. This one was not only extremely attractive but also looked as though she would not be averse to accepting a small gift now and then. Neither Janet nor Verrell had missed, or misunderstood, the gleam in his eyes. Janet was glad — it would not be the first time she had furthered her own interests by leading a man 'up the garden path'. Verrell was worried, since it represented a danger he had not foreseen.

The interview lasted a few minutes only, and was satisfactory to both parties. Mr. Vernon had a new butler and housekeeper; and when the couple had left, Martin's wife gave him a glance that could mean but one thing I His own wife should have been present, but had been prevented by an appointment with her hairdresser — which was, perhaps, just as well!

"Just before you go," Vernon had said in pompous tones, "There is one little point. On no account are you to have your friends in my home. In any case, all guards have been given the strictest instructions never to permit such a thing. As you may have heard, I have a small collection of jewellery" — here he coughed deprecatingly — "and the other day I had an anonymous letter telling me an attempt might be made to steal it. Apparently a fellow called Blackshirt has sworn to do so. Mr. Blackshirt, if he dares to try, will of course end up in gaol- — but as a very slight precaution I must insist on this rule being strictly adhered to. I hope you will both be happy here."

Mrs. Vernon returned two hours after her husband had engaged the new couple. She disliked Verrell on sight, since she saw, or fancied she saw, a gleam of amusement in his eyes when he opened the door to admit her. Since she was wearing a fashion that would have suited a young girl of twenty, perhaps her annoyance was well founded.

That dislike was doubly confirmed when she saw the new housekeeper. She did not consider Janet attractive, but a brazen hussy who must be sent packing at once. Therefore she discharged both servants on the spot. She informed her husband. He promptly took offence and a long row followed, at the tops of their voices; the upshot of it being that the new butler and wife were reinstated. From that moment Mrs. Vernon hated them with every ounce of her small mind.

Verrell was also having his difficulties. In a spirit of carefree gaiety he had entered service. But after he had been engaged he suddenly realized that he should know at least some of the duties of a butler — and beyond the fact that they spoke with grave faces and could indicate the inadequacy of a tip without moving a muscle he was ignorant.

He tackled the question while he was changing. A large room had been allotted them, with two single beds. They arranged to run a curtain of blankets between the two beds at night-time and to take it down as soon as they got up in the morning. There was a small sitting-room leading off the bedroom, where Verrell could dress.

The communicating door was slightly ajar, and Verrell called out, "Janet, what the heck are the duties of a butler?"

There was a moment's silence, then, "First to choose the best Madeira in the cellars and bring it up to here."

"For heaven's sake be sensible. Is it all right for me to come in?"

"Yes."

He entered the bedroom. "Do you know, or don't you?" Janet gurgled at his serious expression. "Richard, I believe you're scared!"

"So I am," he admitted wryly.

"I really can't help you." There was a mischievous expression in her eyes. "The parlour maid will be waiting at table, all you've got to do this evening is to wait on your boss, serve the drinks and carve. It's loin of pork tonight."

"Oh lord!" he groaned. "Carving! Roberts always does that. I have an idea tonight is going to be something!"

It was!

Mrs. Vernon ate in silence, her expression one of grim satisfaction. When Verrell served the red wine cold she could stand it no longer.

"What on earth's this? Damn negligence. Disgraceful." "I — I..." Verrell stammered. His mind had been grappling with future problems and until his employer sat down to table he had forgotten that one of his duties was to take steps to see that the wine was at the correct temperature.

If Mrs. Vernon had refrained from comment the new butler would have been dismissed there and then by an exceedingly irate employer. But she spoke her mind and in doing so reminded him that he had passed Mrs. Martin in the passage earlier that evening and...

"I've never met such incompetence. Edward, this man must go — and his impossible wife."

He glared at her. "Rubbish, my dear. It takes anyone a day or two to get used to things here."

"Edward, I insist!"

"You may go, Martin."

As the butler withdrew, so the argument commenced.

*

On the succeeding days Janet gave her employer several brief opportunities, to which he was not slow to respond. This in turn led to a protest from her 'husband', who felt she was exposing herself to the risk of trouble which might lead to considerable unpleasantness. Janet refused to listen, and pointed out quite logically that, having been around the world, she knew perfectly well how to look after herself.

Verrell discovered that the art of being a good butler could not be acquired by wishful thinking, and he was forced to admit that he only held the position because of Janet. One thing, however, was certain: neither of their employers suspected that they were anything but servants. Both Janet and Verrell had rejected any idea of heavy disguise, but they had dressed and acted, spoken and worked, as though they were used to domestic work and even had Mr. Vernon met them previously it was doubtful whether he would have recognized them.

After they had been at the castle a week, Verrell decided he was ready to proceed with his plans. That night, from his side of the blanket, he outlined his scheme.

"The first thing, Janet, is that I can do nothing unless the safe is open. I've got no more chance of 'cracking' it than flying around this room."

"Don't do that, Richard; after all I'm a poor, defenceless woman in bed!"

151

"Shut up!"

"Yes, sir."

"I managed to get a look at the safe the day before yesterday, when he wanted sandwiches last thing. How the deuce they got it in this place beats me. Whenever he has the safe open there're those two guards outside the door. That means we must tackle at least three men all armed, though 'below-stairs' gossip claims Vernon doesn't know which end of a revolver is which! The whole place is wired up to alarms. On top of that two other guards are patrolling the place, so we have got ourselves a pretty little problem!"

"Giving up, Richard?"

"Of course not! His wife owes me something for all the insults she's hurled at my head," he said laughingly, then continued in a quiet voice, "I'll have to cross from here to the main door, but since I often do that when I take him a late supper it won't occasion any surprise. Then there are the two guards who remain at the top of the staircase. They must be dealt with before they can give the alarm. I dare not risk a sound, for he'd hear it in that inner room of his." "How can you do that?"

"I haven't got that far. The real trouble is going to be making certain that Vernon's got the safe open on the night I decide to act. He's so irregular in the time he spends there." "That's easy," said Janet.

"How so?"

"I'll get him to take me along to see his rings — he's always asking me to. Once he's opened the safe I'll keep him engaged until you turn up."

"Definitely not," he replied sharply.

"Don't be silly. It's the only way."

"I wouldn't Jet you do such a thing. You don't know what might happen when he gets you alone. No, we've got to think of something else."

"Richard I What do you think I am, a Victorian miss? If you can take a risk, so can I." She was angry. The argument was long. And Janet won.

"How are we going to work it?" he asked in a resigned voice.

"You must ask for an evening off. If he thinks you're out of the way, he'll come into the open. His wife is going to see some friends Saturday and staying the night. That will be the best time."

"Allowing that all goes well," Verrell began thoughtfully, "the only people in the keep will be the two guards and Vernon. If we can make certain that they're out of action, there's nothing to stop us walking out of the castle next morning. The guards are relieved at 8 a.m., so any time up till then will be O.K. If we spread around that we're going out for the day, and leaving early, nobody will say a thing."

"The guards might think it funny that you're around if they hear you asked for the night off."

"I doubt it. They'll just reckon I didn't go after all.

Besides, I doubt if they'd look twice at us. We've become one of the normal sights of the castle. They're concerned with the abnormal."

"Richard, there're far too many ifs and ands. Everything seems to be left to chance."

"Not to chance, but to the normal routine of the place."

"I still don't like it. You only came in on this for my sake." Her voice was worried.

"Are you trying to say you want to give up?"

"Yes."

"You're a liar," he stated cheerfully, and switched off the light.

Chapter Sixteen

On Saturday afternoon Mrs. Vernon drove off to visit her friends, not without some qualms about leaving her husband on his own.

As soon as he dared, Vernon sent for the housekeeper on the pretext of discussing the dinner.

Adroitly he changed the conversation. "Would you care, my dear, to come along and see my, ahem! little collection?"

With wide eyes Janet answered, "I'd love to, sir."

"You can call me Edward — that is, when we're alone," he added hastily.

"It will be wonderful, both Mr. Martin and myself have always been very interested in jewels."

"Your husband!" He coughed. "I — I hadn't thought of asking him. When we have finished looking around I thought you might like to choose a little ring, and you know how bored husbands get at such times. No, my dear, let us say it's to be a little party for two."

"But he might object to my coming along alone," she said innocently.

Vernon's expression was not pretty. "Then don't tell him. Suggest he goes to the pictures. I'll see that he has one of the cars."

"It's a funny coincidence, sir — Edward — but George said only yesterday that he wished he could have tonight off to go and see his cousin. The one who's ill."

"Then by all means tell him he has my permission. And there's no need for him to hurry back. Now, my dear, if you come along about midnight"- — here he allowed his arm to rest casually around her shoulders — "I'll arrange everything." He attempted a playful peck at her forehead, which Janet eluded with a light laugh. She returned to her room.

"Twelve o'clock tonight," she told Verrell.

*

Janet was nervous, but when Blackshirt tried to reassure her, she snapped at him. He was dressed in the black jacket he wore as butler, but underneath was wearing the famous black shirt. This he covered with a loose white shirt, which could be removed quickly, as soon as he was in the keep. In a brown-paper parcel he carried a sports jacket which he would put on before Janet and he left early next morning.

At a quarter to twelve Janet left. Blackshirt lit a cigarette. He was to give her ten minutes' start, then follow. Janet was to keep Vernon occupied for half an hour and during that time Blackshirt had to deal with the two guards.

One of the outdoor guards passed Blackshirt as he crossed to the keep. He muttered a good evening, said something about the weather, and then continued on his beat. Blackshirt entered the building, then locked the main door; there was now no fear of interruption. At the foot of the spiral staircase he deposited the paper parcel, and on top of it laid the white shirt. He adjusted the black hood and nylon gloves; then, making sure all was quiet, he started to ascend.

The staircase took a whole turn in about twelve feet so that Blackshirt could get within seven or eight feet of the top without being visible to anyone who happened to be looking down. Half-way between the third and fourth floors a gallery, called the archer's gallery, led off at right angles. This was kept lit, but only by low-wattage bulbs. Blackshirt moved quickly into the gallery and paused. There was no sound of alarm. He switched off the lights and though a faint illumination came from the stairs, it was not sufficient to outline the black shadow standing some four feet inside. From his pocket Blackshirt took out a shilling, through which he had drilled a hole. To this he tied a length of thread. His next move had to wait until one of the guards above moved close to the top of the stairs. He could hear them clearly as they talked.

"Blimey! Jim, where d'you pick this up? Blowed if it ain't the best I've ever seen. That description..." He burst into laughter, in which his companion joined.

"This ain't nothin' compared to the one I lent Bert; that reminds me, the scrounger ain't returned it yet. 'Tain't the first thing he's tried to keep!"

"Aahl" The first man was yawning. There was a quick shuffle of feet as he stood up. "Got any fags on you, Jim? I've run dry. Meant to buy a packet yesterday when I was at the pub."

"You never have got any," was the surly reply. "You still owe me twenty from last Tuesday!"

"Come on, give us one. Call it twenty-one if you like."

"Too ruddy true, I'll call it twenty-one — and you don't get no more 'til I gets the others. Here you are. Now I suppose you want a light?"

"No, I don't. I've got some matches somewhere... That's funny, I thought they were in this pocket... Here what was that?"

There was a 'tinkle, tinkle', as though a coin were falling down the stairs.

"Here, I've dropped something. Must have been that half-crown I thought I'd lost. Hang on to this a moment."

"More like my half-crown, if it is one! Better hurry up, it's still rolling down them stairs."

Hastily the guard descended, his eyes searching the stone steps for the gleam of silver. He was so intent that he did not notice the lights in the gallery were out, but he did see, with an exclamation of satisfaction, a silver coin lying on the steps immediately before the entrance. He bent down to pick it up.

Blackshirt brought the small sand-loaded bag down on his head, and as the man crumpled up, skilfully caught him by his collar and eased the body down on to the ground.

Rapidly Blackshirt arranged the body to make it appear that the man had tripped over and knocked himself unconscious. He descended until he could just see the body round the stairs, then gave a loud cry and brought his foot hard down the edges of three of the steps in a sliding motion.

"Hey, Bert, what's wrong?" Holding his shotgun in both hands the second guard moved slowly downstairs. At the sight of the unconscious Jim he chuckled. "That's what comes of grubbing for money! Too much in a hurry, bet it weren't yours anyway." He bent down and slipped his hands under the unconscious man's armpits.

Without a sound Blackshirt crept up. Three steps... two... one... he had just raised the home-made cosh when the man turned.

Jim dropped the body and made a grab for the gun, at the same time opening his mouth to give the alarm. Blackshirt daren't let the man cry out — at the slightest sound Vernon would take warning. He leaped forward and with one hand covered the man's mouth. With the other he grappled for the gun.

The man was far stronger than he looked. Caring nothing for the blows Blackshirt aimed at his head he heaved himself forward until his right hand was almost on the trigger-guard; at the same time he bit down on Blackshirt's hand.

Blackshirt brought the edge of his hand down on the man's forefinger as it groped for the trigger. The blow took effect just below the joint which was resting on the trigger-guard. The guard gasped with pain as the bone snapped. Reversing his tactics he brought his knee hard up into Blackshirt's stomach, and had he not rolled half sideways off, that blow would have finished the fight — as it was it brought tears to his eyes. Ignoring the pain Blackshirt slapped the man beneath the nose with his right hand, and jerked his left into the other's Adam's apple. For a split second he was able to roll free. The sand-bag was some three feet away where he had dropped it. With one movement he brought it up... and down on the man's head. Without a sound Jim lost consciousness.

Blackshirt stood up panting. His stomach felt as though it were bruised all over, and his left hand was painful, though the glove had to some extent protected his flesh. Allowing three minutes to shake off the effects, he lifted each man, bound and gagged them in turn and left them in the gallery.

He looked at his watch. It was thirty minutes since he had left the room. Ten minutes more than Janet and he had allowed.

*

Vernon was perplexed. In his limited imagination the evening's entertainment should have proceeded far more smoothly. A quick glance at his collection, and Mrs. Martin would choose a ring, a small one. He would give it to her with many flowery compliments. And then...

But Mrs. Martin was not content just to be shown a few of the safe's contents. She insisted on a thorough examination, and, as she exclaimed delightedly over the finer pieces, an amazed employer realized he was dealing with a woman who knew the worth of jewellery. Two or three times he had tried to bring her enjoyment to an end, but each time she either took no notice, or laughed softly and continued. He was fast losing patience.

"My dear, if you will make your choice, we can move into the next room and have some sherry. You'd like some, wouldn't you?"

"No thanks," replied a wide-eyed Janet. "My husband doesn't believe in my drinking — and, besides, it's far more exciting here."

Never had she seen such diamonds, such strings of pearls. It *was* a fabulous collection, even larger than she had believed. No taste was evident in its arrangement. As each new piece arrived it must have been put in the nearest empty space, with the result that the whole looked theatrical and false.

"I'm afraid, my dear, we can't spend any more time here, it's getting late."

Janet looked at her watch. It was already just after half past twelve, and Blackshirt should have arrived some time ago.

"Make your choice from this lot!" There was an edge to his voice, almost a command, that warned her she could draw out the proceedings no longer. Could Blackshirt have failed? she wondered. Had he been captured by the guards?

"From these, you said?"

"Certainly. You wouldn't want anything larger, would you? Might not be quite suitable."

Janet held back a giggle at the idea of a housekeeper wearing one of the rings she was being offered; none of them was worth less than five hundred pounds.

"How about this one? Seems to suit you very well." He slipped it on to her third finger.

"It does, doesn't it?"

Vernon started. For a ghastly moment he thought his wife had returned, but, realizing that it was a man's voice, he turned. "How dare you..."

His lower jaw sagged as he saw Blackshirt standing three feet outside the door of the safe, a shotgun in his hands. Whatever else he might be, Vernon was no coward, and he called out to the guards.

Blackshirt shook his head in sympathy. "I'm afraid they won't hear you. And if you move your hand any nearer that pocket, I shall be forced to pull one or both of these triggers."

"Who are you — what do you want?"

"If my name interests you, it's Blackshirt."

"Blackshirt!"

"Precisely."

"Damn you! You'll never get away with it. You'll never get out of here, you fool! Listen, if you go now, I'll promise on my word of honour to let you go through the gates unharmed. I don't care to see any man go to gaol, but if you don't accept my offer, that's where you'll end." There was panic in his voice. Only too clearly he appreciated the threat to his beloved collection.

As his words had no effect, he continued wildly, "Look here, if you'll promise to leave, I'll pay you. Much more than you'd ever get from these few things. You could retire and become an honest man!"

"How will you pay me?"

Hope appeared in Vernon's eyes. "By cheque, of course. Three thousand pounds' — four thousand pounds." He increased his offer wildly.

"Come on, Blackshirt, stop playing with the little man. Let's hurry up." Janet spoke for the first time.

Vernon swore as he realized how easily the whole affair had been managed. Playing on his emotions they had outwitted him until it looked as though nothing could prevent them taking whatever they wished from his safe.

"And to think I was warned against you," he muttered.

Disregarding his misery, Blackshirt handed the gun over to Janet before running a practised hand over his employer. He found a small automatic which he put in his pocket. Then, with an ironic apology, he bound, but did not gag, his victim.

"Where are they?" asked Blackshirt eagerly.

"I can't see them anywhere," said Janet, in a worried voice, "and I've looked over most of the stuff."

Blackshirt turned to Vernon. "To save a lot of time and trouble, where have you put the Darthweight pearls?"

"You damned scoundrel," the millionaire spluttered, "not content with assaulting me you accuse me of receiving stolen goods. I'll see you get gaoled for life if it's the last thing I do!"

Blackshirt ignored the heated outburst. "You paid sixty thousand pounds for them."

"Since you know so damned much, why don't you find them for yourself."

Wasting no more time, Blackshirt searched the safe. He looked through shelf after shelf marvelling, as Janet had done, at the incredible display of gems, but nowhere could he find what he sought. Was it possible that Otto had been wrong? It had been pure guess work. A feeling of anti-climax assailed him. It seemed he had made a mistake. True, there were more precious stones within reach than he had ever seen in one place before, but he was after the Darthweight pearls — and they were all that mattered!

Then he realized a significant fact — not one of the jewels he had seen was, so to speak, 'contraband'. He knew of a number of pieces of jewellery which Vernon was reputed to have obtained by illegal methods; they were all missing.

"Where do you keep the rest of your collection?"

A flicker of apprehension in Vernon's eyes proved Blackshirt's guess correct.

"I — I don't know what you mean."

"Would it be at the back of this safe?"

"Would what be at the back?" But again the swift gleam in his eyes told Blackshirt he was right.

"Where's the key — or is it a combination?"

"I don't know what the devil you are referring to. For God's sake take what you've come for and go." He strained at the bonds in a futile effort to free himself.

Blackshirt realized that no matter what he did, what threats he used, the other would never disclose the secret of the second safe.

"Janet, give me a hand. We'll see if we can discover whereabouts it is."

The two moved to the far end of the safe. The wall was unbroken by shelving, and apparently consisted of a solid block of metal. But somewhere along it, if his theory was correct, must be the outline of a door. It took them several minutes of laborious searching before Janet finally discovered a minute crack in the metal. It was a miracle of workmanship, so closely did the two parts fit into one another.

"Now what?" asked a discouraged Janet.

"There must be a locking mechanism, somewhere in the centre. If it's one-tenth as complicated as the main door we haven't a hope; but my guess is that, since it's only an auxiliary safe already protected by the outside door, it won't be.

He searched again, and at last outlined a further break in the middle.

"This is it, but how the deuce does it open?" Painstakingly he explored the surrounding surface. At one point the metal gave and there was a click. A dial combination and handle were revealed.

Blackshirt set to work. He unwrapped a stethoscope, and, having fitted it to his ears, held the trumpet to the lock with his left hand, and twirled the dials with his right. Janet watched, enthralled by her companion's delicate touch and concentrated patience.

Thirty minutes passed; an hour; two hours... by which time his hood was stained with sweat, and his muscles painful. At last he stood up to ease his limbs, turning towards Janet as he did so. He looked dispirited.

"No luck so far! How's the time? Afraid it's going to beat me."

"Four already. We can't give up now, Blackshirt' — I tell you what, the old boy offered me a sherry, it's all ready in the next room. Let's go and have a quick one."

Blackshirt took the opportunity of making certain that the two guards were still securely bound. Both had recovered consciousness. When he returned to the library Janet took a cigarette from a box on the table and lit it for him. She insisted he sat down whilst she poured out a sherry.

After fifteen minutes, Blackshirt resumed his slow work. The minutes passed, still without result; and not until halfpast five, when he had set himself a limit of another thirty minutes, did he at last obtain the combination. With a sigh of relief he swung open the door.

The second safe was a miniature of the first. A quarter of the size, it was lined on all three sides in the same manner. As Blackshirt walked around, he recognized gem after gem which had been stolen and never traced: some he himself had handled.

Janet joined him.

"Have you found them?"

"Over there." He pointed to the far wall.

Once again Janet had possession of the Darthweight pearls, but with a mischievous smile she wandered around, helping herself to some of the choicest pieces. Blackshirt watched her with cynical amusement. He had been after the pearls, and he had got them. The rest did not interest him, and he was perfectly prepared to let Edward Vernon keep it.

By the time Janet had made her choice it was close on six. They moved back to the library, but not before Janet had shown Vernon precisely what she was taking. Verrell laughed at his agonized expression. He made one last impassioned plea, but Janet lightly kissed her fingers and said if she heard any more she'd return to the safe.

At five to seven they left the library and walked down to the main door, where Blackshirt picked up the paper parcel. He entered one of the adjoining rooms for a few moments, then returned wearing the white shirt and sports jacket.

"Ready, Janet?" he asked.

"Yes."

He took her arm as they left the keep and Janet realized what nerves of steel Blackshirt must have. She felt an almost unmanageable desire to increase her pace and get out of the castle grounds as quickly as possible. But her companion continued at the deliberate pace he had used whilst in 'service'. And all the time he chatted away with suggestions as to where they might spend the day.

Fifty yards from the heavy wooden door, which was kept locked at night, the gatekeeper saw them and limped out to open up.

At the same moment a horn sounded imperiously from outside and as the gate opened a car drove in. Mrs. Vernon had returned.

Chapter Seventeen

The car drew abreast of Janet and Blackshirt and then came to a halt. Mrs. Vernon leant out.

"Where are you two going?" she asked in a shrill voice. "We're going out for the day, madam," replied Verrell suavely.

"Who said you could have the day off — I didn't!"

"Mr. Vernon, madam. My cousin is ill and I requested that my wife and I should be allowed to go and see him."

"Umph!" She seemed annoyed that she could find no fault. She was staring at the *petite* form of Janet with suspicion and envy when her expression hardened.

"What's that on your finger?"

Janet looked down. She was still wearing the ring that Vernon had slipped on her finger earlier that night. She cursed her stupidity.

"Well, what is it?" Mrs. Vernon repeated loudly.

"A ring madam. One my husband gave me when we were engaged."

Mrs. Vernon caught hold of Janet's arm and forced it up so that she could see the ring more clearly. "You lying hussy! I recognize it — that's one of mine. Where did you get it?" She raised her voice; shouted "Thieves! Close the gates. Jenkins, catch her." This to one of the guards who had drawn near from curiosity.

Blackshirt quickly gauged his chances. The gateman was blocking the only exit from the courtyard, the nearby guard was still hesitant, bemused by the sudden sequence of events. A third man, attracted by the shrill shout, was running towards the car from the direction of the stables. Only one avenue of escape from immediate arrest remained, and that was but a temporary expedient.

Grasping Janet firmly he freed her from the clutch of the semi-hysterical woman; then together they raced for the keep. As he slammed the door to, and locked it, an alarm-bell in the tower above the portcullis sent the echo of its deep call vibrating across the quiet countryside.

"I'm — I'm sorry," gasped Janet, in a very small voice, her lower lip quivering. "If only I'd noticed…"

" 'If ifs and ands,' " quoted Blackshirt cheerfully. Inwardly he was feeling anything but cheerful: he knew that a call would already have gone through to the local police station, that within six minutes or so the police would be there, that the one and only exit from the keep would be guarded by armed men. They were caught like rats in a trap.

His thoughts raced as he tried to find a way out of their predicament.

"Mr. Edward Vernon's got the last laugh after all." Janet made a brave attempt to smile.

"Not yet" denied Blackshirt. "While there's life… Quick, up to the top as fast as you can go." He led the way, taking three steps at a time.

Vernon lay where they had left him, but his mouth curled in a vicious smile when he saw them enter.

"That looks like the end of you, Mr. Cocksure Blackshirt. In about ten minutes from now the police will put you where you belong. I shall see you get more than the last fool got!"

For the moment Blackshirt ignored him. "Janet, go to the window and keep an eye open for the police. As soon as they come yell out. The guards won't do anything till they arrive."

Janet raced off down the stairs. Though she could see no way out, yet her faith in Blackshirt's ingenuity was such that she obeyed him without question.

"Trying to prolong your last taste of liberty," sneered Vernon.

"What will they do when they catch me?" asked Blackshirt, in an unhurried tone of voice.

Vernon laughed harshly. "What do you think they'll do, you fool? First thing they'll search you and recover everything you've stolen "

"Precisely!" Blackshirt's voice betrayed considerable satisfaction.

"Eh? What do you mean?"

"You know what we've taken?"

"Of course I do. Apart from anything else you've robbed me of the Darthweight pearls — the pearls…!" The words tailed away into silence.

Blackshirt grinned. "See what I mean. They'll discover that you're a receiver of stolen property. I think you'll find the police will be just as interested in you as they are in me — particularly when I tell them about the inside safe!"

The man on the floor winced. Now, not only was his beloved collection threatened, but so was his own liberty. He looked up at Blackshirt with a mixture of fear and cunning.

"Can't you do something? Try and escape. I'll say nothing, I swear I won't. Don't just stand here… Try something. Try anything."

"Are you ready to do as I tell you?"

"Yes — yes. Anything you say."

Blackshirt bent down and unbound him. He helped Vernon to his feet and slapped his limbs to restore the circulation. "I don't know what yet. But if I do think of something, and you don't help us, we're in this together. Just remember that."

"How the devil can I forget it?" groaned Vernon, in the added agony of returning circulation.

They were startled by a shout from Janet.

"Blackshirt, the police I The gates are being opened. A car's coming in." There was the suspicion of a sob in her voice.

Blackshirt hurried to the window and looked down at the courtyard nearly fifty feet below. Mrs. Vernon's old-fashioned car was standing where she had ordered the chauffeur to pull up... he could hear the sweet throb of the engine still ticking over. The chauffeur, however, had left the car, to cluster with the rest of the staff about the main door of the keep, which they thumped and kicked in the apparent belief that mere noise was a key to open it.

Approaching the door was a long, sleek police car, and behind it moved a motor-cycle mounted by a leather-booted, crash-helmeted constable. Across the courtyard the porter was once more closing the gates which he had opened to give entry to the police. Janet and Blackshirt were still gazing down at the busy scene as the police car came to a screeching halt, and an inspector and two constables leaped out. The motor-cycle pulled up alongside, but at a signal from the inspector its rider remained mounted.

"Not taking any chances," muttered Blackshirt.

"It's hopeless," Janet wailed. "Oh, Blackshirt! This time we've really had it."

For the moment he did not answer; he was fascinated by the sight of the Vernon's car some eight yards from the keep door, its engine still running.

"If only we could reach that car, Janet..."

"How could we? With all those men?"

"Yes, but if?"

"What would be the use? The gates are closed. It's hopeless. We might as well surrender... and it's all my fault! Oh!"

"The gates are only of wood. That heavy saloon would crash through them like a tank."

"Even if we could, how far would we get? That police car could run circles round the other. We wouldn't get a mile before they caught us."

Blackshirt swallowed. "No," he muttered. "I'm just dreaming. As you say, old girl, we've had it." And then, gleefully, triumphantly, "Eureka!"

"What is it, Richard?"

"Listen… "

*

"What's the trouble, madam?" asked the inspector. They had been called out twice before — on a wild goose chase, and the police of the district privately consigned Vernon and his collection to the nether regions.

"The housekeeper stole one of my rings. Stole it!" Mrs. Vernon accused savagely. "You must arrest her at once, Inspector, I insist."

"Where is she?" he asked wearily.

"Up there," interrupted the nearest guard, foreseeing his employer would continue in the same strain for a long time. "She was caught leaving with her husband — the butler — and both of them dashed back." He pointed to the keep.

The inspector looked up. Just then Vernon leant out of a window on the third floor. He waved his arms excitedly. "Help. Quick. They're up here. They've opened the safe.

For heaven's sake get a move on before they take anything more."

"Door's locked," reported an unemotional constable.

"Have you a key?" the inspector shouted up. In answer Vernon hurriedly threw down a key.

"Watch the door, they may try to make a break for it. You two come up," the inspector told the other policemen.

Followed by his men, the inspector hurried up the stairs. On the third floor a wild-eyed and dishevelled Vernon met them. Janet was with him, handcuffed to his right wrist.

"The man's somewhere on the roof. Drew a gun on me and threatened to shoot me if I stood in his way. But I've got the woman. You go and get him." The police moved off. "Inspector — Inspector…"

"What is it?" the inspector asked angrily, already halfway up to the next floor.

"The guard's been knocked out. I can't get him off the floor: looks as though he's hurt. Can someone give me a hand?"

"Go to the devil," muttered the inspector under his breath. Aloud, "Smither, give Mr. Vernon a hand. We'll deal with the butler."

166

"Where is the guard?" asked the constable, as the others disappeared.

"Over there."

A figure was stretched out on the floor. Smither bent down and, putting his arms around the middle of the unconscious man, lifted him off the ground in a fireman's hoist. With an effort he straightened himself.

"Where to, sir?" he panted.

"Take him down to Mrs. Vernon's car. The chauffeur can drive him to the hospital. I'll follow with the prisoner. Hurry, man, hurry."

"I'm hurrying best I can, sir. This ain't no feather I'm carrying."

They reached the keep door. When Mrs. Vernon saw Janet handcuffed to her husband's wrist she laughed loudly.

"So, my fine lady, you'd steal my rings would you."

"Let her be," Vernon snapped. "We've got to get Williams to the hospital." He pushed his wife aside, then cleared a path through the staff.

"Drop him in the back seat," Vernon ordered as they reached the saloon.

The constable did so. As he stood upright with a sigh of relief and began mopping his forehead, things happened. There was a bellow from the roof of the keep. The injured man sat upright; gave the constable a thrust which sent the unfortunate man reeling backwards across the cobbled courtyard. Simultaneously, Janet released her hand from the handcuff and slipped into the driving seat. The wail of gears rose to a high crescendo as she stamped on the accelerator. The heavy saloon moved ponderously forward towards the exit.

But neither the driver of the police car nor the motorcyclist were blind, or fools. Something was wrong. Their engines roared into life, and their gears screeched as they swung around and followed in the track of the saloon. Only a matter of yards separated the cycle from the saloon as the latter charged into the archway of the gatehouse. Janet brought the car to a rocking halt as Blackshirt leaned out of the window, and with a sharp knife from his belt of tools hacked away at the rope securing the portcullis. Two... four... six... and then the last remaining strand.

"Now," he yelled.

Janet revved furiously. The old saloon leaped forward beneath the descending portcullis. There was a heavy thump as the iron base of the portcullis struck the ground; a second thump as the motor-cyclist charged headlong into it; and finally the crash of rending timber as the saloon smashed through the wooden gate at the other end of the arched passage.

Blackshirt gazed through the rear window, and grinned. By the time the police had raised the portcullis Janet and he would be miles away...

"Up the good old days!" he shouted in happy abandon.

"Nearly eight o'clock.' Verrell remarked. "How about coming back to the flat and having some breakfast? I need something to take away the taste of the past few days. Yes, madam. No, madam! "

She laughed. "You wouldn't make a butler in a thousand years! Breakfast by all means, after which I must return to the hotel. Richard, I do wish we could have brought away more than we did."

"Seems to me I'm lucky you didn't try to take the safe!"

By nine o'clock they were both sitting in his lounge enjoying coffee and hot buttered rolls. At nine-fifteen Verrell excused himself, saying he wanted to change. Leaving Janet contentedly smoking a cigarette he entered his bedroom, and shut the door.

At nine-eighteen Verrell removed the Roselea rubies from his right-hand pocket, and hid them under his pillow. He was glad he had had first chance to walk around the safe!

Chapter Eighteen

At nine-thirty, Verrell returned to the sitting-room. The party had increased by one — Peebles lounged in a chair with a smirk on his face.

" 'Morning, Blackshirt. Been having a busy time I hear! Jim told me it was on the eight o'clock news. The one and only Blackshirt — a butler!" He chuckled. "How did you make out?"

"Lousy," muttered Janet, who was fidgeting.

"I take my hat off to you! Damned if I don't. It would take more nerve than I've got to do what you've just done. Incidentally, what was it worth?"

"What was what worth?" Verrell replied easily.

"Do you mean to say you didn't get the Darthweight pearls?" he asked in surprise. "I only sold them to Vernon three weeks ago. Dear me, to think what you've missed!" There was silence as Peebles gazed from one to the other. Then, "Where were you going when I arrived, Janet?"

"None of your business."

"And in such a hurry," he continued mockingly. "As I came up the stairs, Blackshirt, she was just about to leave at top speed. Impulsive little creature, isn't she? I bet you had no idea she was going so soon!"

Verrell remained silent. He didn't doubt that Peebles was telling the truth, that Janet had been on the point once again of disappearing with the hard-won pearls; Janet's vicious glare was ample confirmation. It hurt him that even now she couldn't play straight. Admittedly he had not yet told her about the Roselea rubies, but he had intended to produce them as a surprise.

His thoughts were all too clearly mirrored in his eyes and for a brief moment Janet felt forlorn. She would have given all she had to see the one expression in his eyes that she knew now she would never see. She wasted no time in vain regrets. If she knew her Peebles he had not come on a social visit. Opening her bag as though looking for a handkerchief, Janet whipped out a small revolver and covered the two men. "Just in case you're thinking of trying anything — don't!" She paused, then, "It's probably the last time I shall ever see either of you. As far as you, Peebles, are concerned, I couldn't care less — I've always despised you."

He swore and moved in his chair, but at a movement from the revolver relaxed.

"Blackshirt, I like and admire. But the two of you together aren't clever enough for one woman." Her voice was sharp. She was fighting her own feelings.

"This time tomorrow I shall be out of the country. Well away from either of you, so maybe in future you will be able to keep what you take! In any case, this is good-bye." She looked at Peebles for a second, then stared at Blackshirt. Something welled from the corner of each eye. The next second she had slipped through the door.

Peebles did not stay much longer. For once he was in a quiet mood and when he left, declining an invitation to lunch, he shook hands with Verrell.

Absent-mindedly Verrell picked up a scrap of waste-paper from the floor, then poured himself out a drink and relaxed in his favourite armchair. The past week had been fun and had more than satisfied his love of excitement. Indeed, ever since the night he had won — and lost — at roulette, events had followed one another with joyous rapidity. But it all added up to the unpalatable truth that he had lost — and heavily. Janet had won! It was illogical that, knowing her character so well, he should be upset by her latest betrayal. If she had wanted the jewels so much she could have said so… and he would have given them to her. Now, if he had the chance, he would do his utmost to regain them. Whereabouts would he find Janet? Only one thing was certain: she would not have returned to her hotel. With a grin he realized that probably the cashier, also, might like to locate her, since it was odds on that her bill was outstanding.

Verrell withdrew his hand from his pocket and regarded the crumpled scrap of paper he had been unconsciously twiddling. Where had it come from? He remembered; it was the piece he had automatically picked up from the floor. Looking closer, he saw it contained a list that could be a time-table.

Times for what? he wondered idly. The writing was not his, nor Robert's — then whose was it? He grew excited. What if it were Janet's. Something she had dropped from her bag. Roberts would have swept up the previous day, so that it could only have belonged to someone present that morning. And as he thought back, he realized that Peebles had never been in that part of the room.

What times were they? Trains or boats was his immediate answer. 0930, D.C., 1300, F.C., 0905, N.D., 2100, S.H. D.C… For a time he was puzzled

170

by the letters, and could make nothing of them. D.C... F.C... Then he had an idea. D.C... Dover.Calais? N.D... New-haven.Dieppe? With mounting excitement he reached for the latest British-Railways time-table of cross-Channel routes. Were there any services corresponding to the figures on the list? Too late now, for the Dover.Calais route. Southampton was a night route only. To his joy Folkestone agreed. The time was just after a quarter past ten. If Janet were, in fact, using that route, she would probably catch the 1300 train. But she had no passport! Then he remembered Peebles had returned it as soon as he had sold the pearls.

He would reach Folkestone in just over two hours by car if he really drove, and still have time — but once there what exactly could he do?

Quickly he walked round to the lock-up garage he used, filled up with petrol, and drove southwards as rapidly as he dared.

*

"Then George, he's my cousin, wanted to see whether Ethel..."

Janet stared out of the window of the train, and let the interminable saga of the woman's life flow over her head. The train was due in at Folkestone at any moment. Despite the fact that none was aware when or by which route she was leaving England, she had a nagging sense of insecurity.

The train pulled in at the harbour station and Janet stepped on to the platform. Carefully she scanned the crowds. She could recognize no one, and breathed more freely.

"Porter, miss?"

"Yes, please. Just the two bags in here. I have a cabin on the boat."

"Right you are, miss, number 361 is me number. Got to go through the customs first, but we'll see if I can't get you through quick."

"Thank you," she replied absently, as she walked along the platform in the direction of the customs shed.

The porter was as good as his word. Using the bags as a ram he forced a passage through the crowds, who made way. Janet followed close behind.

"Here we are, miss. If I tip this officer the wink, he'll get you through soon as he's finished with the party in yellow." He called out, but 'the customs officer took no notice; he was busily occupied in answering a traveller who wanted to know how many dozen bottles of wine he could bring back from the Continent duty-free.

A hoarse gargle, then a spit as the porter cleared his throat sufficiently to enjoy a cigarette. A thin, drooping, home-rolled sent a column of smoke aloft to drift round a 'No Smoking' sign.

"How much money have you?" inquired the customs official in a bored voice as he moved along the table. "May I see your passport, please."

Janet handed it over. He examined the currency page, then turned to the front.

"Are you Miss Dove?"

"Yes."

"Miss Janet Dove?"

"Of course, that's what my passport says," she replied sharply.

"Yes, quite. I would like to examine your luggage, please. Put it here," he told the porter. "Are these two suitcases your only luggage?"

"Yes." Janet was worried. The man's manner had changed from that of someone doing a routine job to one of alertness tinged with a trace of suspicion. She had thought at the time that he stressed her name, but had not paid particular attention to the fact. Was it possible that he was about to search for the jewels — that he knew she had them with her?

"Would you unlock them, please? You know that you are only allowed five pounds in notes?"

"Of course."

"And you have no more than that?"

"I have only two pounds, and a small amount of silver."

"Very well. This bag first, if you don't mind." Carefully, but quickly, he emptied the case, unrolling each article of clothing as he did so.

"May I ask what you are looking for?" She kept her voice even.

"We've had notice that a female passenger answering your description is trying to take a large sum in notes over to the Continent."

"But that's absurd! I've already told you I've only two pounds."

"Sorry, but it's my job to make sure."

Janet was worried — and relieved. Worried that someone had informed the customs, since it meant he had known her movements; relieved that the jewels were on her person. If the customs had found them, there would have been trouble with a capital T, since she would have been breaking the law by attempting to export undeclared jewellery — and the police would only too soon realize where it had come from.

The first bag was cleared after an expert examination for secret pockets. Soon the other likewise.

"Now, miss, I'll have to ask you to come over with me. We have a woman searcher who will tell you what to do. Follow me, please. The porter will bring the bags along."

172

A moment's panic that had to be quickly subdued. A personal search — inevitably the jewels would be found! She did not argue, but followed the official as he came from behind the trestle table and led the way to the far comer of the shed.

Janet's face was expressionless; her mind grappling with the problem that had so suddenly arisen.

She sneezed, stopped walking, and sneezed again. Opening her bag Janet felt for a handkerchief. She found none, nor in the pocket of her dress.

"I must get a handkerchief — from the blue case."

The customs man turned, and his expression hardened. Janet felt herself go cold. If her sleight-of-hand were not quick enough she would be detected there and then, but it was her only chance.

"Kindly give me the keys. Put the bag down here," said the officer to the porter. "This bag, I think you said." He opened it.

Janet knelt down to take out a handkerchief, realizing as she did so that she dare not transfer the jewels to the bag. The officer was watching her too keenly.

"Gent there waving to you, him with three stripes?" mumbled the porter, removing a battered stub of cigarette from his mouth to make himself more coherent.

The other looked up briefly. "Better get a new pair of eyes, chum, he's not waving at anyone. Now, miss, if you'll take your handkerchief, we'll move on so that you'll have time to catch the boat."

Janet removed the top article, a thin summer coat, and then took a handkerchief from a small pile. She blew her nose. The officer's suspicions were stilled, since it was impossible that she could have deposited anything in the bag while he was watching.

At the hut they halted.

"Come with me, please. The porter will wait here for you."

Some fifteen minutes later Janet reappeared. There was a brief apology for having troubled her. She replied with a note of annoyance in her voice.

"Sorry, Miss Dove, but we've all got our job to do. If you hurry you'll be able to get a seat in the lounge."

"It's all right, thank you, I have a cabin. Porter, bring the bags along. I want Cabin Z."

They were aboard none too soon. Already the breast-ropes were being cast off.

The porter stowed the bags on the floor. Janet handed him five shillings, whereupon he touched his cap and left.

*

The sea was calm. The cabin door locked. The window curtained. With a feeling of ease, delightful release from the strain that had for so long restricted her thoughts and actions, Janet unlocked her blue case. The small wash-leather bag that had caused so much trouble was hidden in the folds of the coat on top.

She unfolded the coat and took out the bag — empty. Her mind refused to take in the fact. For fully thirty seconds she gazed in disbelief.

There was a piece of paper sticking out of the top; hardly realizing what she was doing, she opened the bag and pulled it out.

Thanks, Janet, for everything — including the generous tip which no doubt you will give me before we part.

Love, No. 361.

If you enjoyed *Blackshirt Wins the Trick*, please share your thoughts on Amazon by leaving a review.

For more free and discounted eBooks every week, sign up to the Endeavour Press newsletter.

Follow us on Twitter and Instagram.

Printed in Great Britain
by Amazon